"Do you really believe I am in danger?"

Paloma felt sick when Daniele nodded. The idea that someone valued her inheritance and control of the company more than her life was a crushing blow to her already-shaky self-esteem. "Marriage to me could put your life in danger. Why would you be prepared to risk your safety?" she asked Daniele huskily.

"My final words to your grandfather before he died were a promise to protect you. Like you, I have no wish to marry, but I'm afraid there is no other way."

Daniele could not have made it any clearer that he would prefer to walk barefoot through a pit of vipers than walk up the aisle with her. His incentive was that she was the Morante heiress, and he hoped that by marrying her, he would gain his mother's acceptance.

Paloma stared at the ring he had placed on her finger. An engagement ring was meant to be a symbol of love and commitment, but for all its beauty, the sapphire ring was a reminder of the marriage bargain she had made with a man who regarded her as his duty and nothing more.

Chantelle Shaw lives on the Kent coast and thinks up her stories while walking on the beach. She has been married for over thirty years and has six children. Her love affair with reading and writing Harlequin stories began as a teenager, and her first book was published in 2006. She likes strong-willed, slightly unusual characters. Chantelle also loves gardening, walking and wine.

Books by Chantelle Shaw

Harlequin Presents

The Virgin's Sicilian Protector
Reunited by a Shock Pregnancy
Wed for the Spaniard's Redemption
Proof of Their Forbidden Night
Her Wedding Night Negotiation
Housekeeper in the Headlines

Innocent Summer Brides

The Greek Wedding She Never Had
Nine Months to Tame the Tycoon

Visit the Author Profile page
at Harlequin.com for more titles.

Chantelle Shaw

THE ITALIAN'S BARGAIN
FOR HIS BRIDE

HARLEQUIN
PRESENTS

ISBN-13: 978-1-335-56928-8

The Italian's Bargain for His Bride

This edition published by arrangement with Harlequin Books S.A.

For questions and comments about the quality of this book, please contact us at CustomerService@Harlequin.com.

Harlequin Enterprises ULC
22 Adelaide St. West, 40th Floor
Toronto, Ontario M5H 4E3, Canada
www.Harlequin.com

Printed in U.S.A.

THE ITALIAN'S BARGAIN
FOR HIS BRIDE

PROLOGUE

'PALOMA IS A RISK!'

Franco Zambrotta slammed his hand down on the desk.

'She has spent most of her life in England, disconnected from her Italian heritage. Her ill-advised marriage swiftly followed by a divorce proved that she is headstrong. In my opinion, Marcello's granddaughter is not suitable to take charge of Morante Group. I am sure I do not need to remind you, Daniele, that the company is a global brand with a multibillion-dollar annual revenue. It cannot be entrusted to a girl who has no experience of running a business.'

'With respect, Franco, your opinion on this matter is irrelevant.' Daniele Berardo spoke in his customary, calm manner, hiding his dislike of the other man. It amazed him that Marcello Morante, the founder of Morante Group, who had been renowned for his charisma as much as for his brilliant business acumen, had been related to the distinctly charmless Franco.

In the past twenty-four hours since Marcello had collapsed on the golf course and died on the way to the hospital, Daniele hadn't had a chance to assimilate the loss of the man who had been his mentor and close friend. His priority was to ensure that the media did not learn of Marcello's death before his granddaughter had been informed. But Paloma Morante, the sole heiress to her grandfather's vast fortune, had disappeared.

The conversation with the man Paloma called Great-Uncle Franco was pointless and a waste of Daniele's time when he urgently needed to find her, but his enigmatic expression revealed none of his frustration as he said imperturbably, 'It was Marcello's wish that Paloma would eventually succeed him. However, he stipulated in his will that if he died before his granddaughter was twenty-five, Morante Group must be managed by the board of trustees until Paloma comes of age to take control of the company. Do I need to remind you, Franco, that your duty as the president of the board is to work in collaboration with the other trustees and run Morante Group until Paloma's twenty-fifth birthday?'

Franco snorted. 'Several of the board members have expressed their concern that Paloma lacks the qualities of leadership. I intend to call for a vote of no confidence in her and propose that I am instated as Marcello's permanent successor.'

The imperceptible tightening of Daniele's jaw was the only indication that he was disturbed by Franco's threat of a power struggle. He had never trusted Marcello's much younger half-brother. Franco was the product of their mother's second marriage after Marcello's father had died relatively young, it was rumoured from a drug overdose. Marcello had been the sole Morante heir and later had given his half-brother a senior role in the company. Admittedly, Paloma's only experience of working at Morante Group had been during a gap year while she had been at university. It was possible that Franco would win a majority vote from the board of trustees to displace her. Daniele recalled the last words Marcello had said to him.

'Will you promise to take care of my grand-daughter? I have come to regard you as the grandson I never had, Daniele. I beg you to think of Paloma as your sister and protect her from the sharks who will want a piece of her when I have gone.'

How was he supposed to think of Paloma as his sister? Daniele wondered grimly. He had tried not to think about her at all for the past three years.

Paloma had been a coltish teenager the first time he had met her, although even then she had shown signs that she would be a great beauty. Daniele had noticed her, but he had been trying to rebuild his life and hadn't paid her much attention.

When Paloma was twenty-one, she had come to Livorno on the west coast of Tuscany to take up an internship with Morante Group. The luxury leather goods business had grown to be a market leader, in part due to Daniele, who had established the company's online presence.

Daniele had been blown away by the beautiful young woman Paloma had become. He pictured her slender figure, chestnut-brown hair and milky pale skin as perfect as the finest porcelain. Paloma possessed an inherent elegance that spoke of her aristocratic heritage spread across three European countries. Her grandfather was a marchese. Marcello's wife, who had died tragically young, had been the daughter of a French duke, and Paloma's English mother was linked, albeit distantly, to the British royal family.

Daniele had found it impossible to resist the chemistry that had flared between him and Paloma. He had tried to keep his distance, conscious that he was twelve years older than her, and his position on the board of Morante Group made him her superior at work.

But on the night of a grand ball held in Marcello's opulent palazzo, Paloma had flirted with him, and when she had instigated a kiss, Daniele's self-control had cracked, and he'd succumbed to her sensual allure. He could still recall how soft her lips had felt beneath his. But he had been brought to his senses by the certainty that her grandfather would not have approved. Marcello had often spoken of his hope that Paloma would make a good marriage within the Italian nobility.

Daniele had not seen Paloma since that night when he had rejected her, but he had often found himself thinking about her. She had lodged like a bur in his skin, and for the past three years, his fascination with her had not faded. However, he was determined to keep his promise to Marcello to act like a brother to Paloma. But first he had to find her and break the terrible news that her grandfather had died.

He knew she lived in London, where she kept a low profile. She had adamantly refused her grandfather's plea to have a bodyguard. But Marcello's death meant that Paloma was a billionairess. Her life was going to be different from now on, and she would have to accept the protection of a security team.

Daniele had been given Paloma's contact details by Marcello's PA, but her mobile phone was switched off. When he'd called her landline number, he had been informed by her flatmate that Paloma was away at a yoga retreat somewhere in Ireland.

'Paloma should be here at Morante Group's

headquarters.' Franco's terse voice interrupted Daniele's thoughts. 'You asked me to delay making a formal announcement of Marcello's death to give his granddaughter time to prepare for the inevitable media attention. But I will not wait any longer and risk the news being leaked to the press. Strong leadership is vital at this time.'

'You must understand that Paloma is shocked and distressed.' Daniele was sure she would be devastated, but he was not going to admit to Franco that he did not know her whereabouts, or that Paloma was still unaware of Marcello's death. 'I insist that she must be given more time to come to terms with her loss. Only the board of trustees and a handful of medical staff who treated Marcello know he is dead. I have taken out a legal injunction to prevent anyone talking to the media without my permission.'

'You had no right to go behind my back,' Franco said furiously.

'I had to act quickly to ensure the stability of the company. Marcello appointed me as lifelong vice president of the board in recognition of my loyalty to him and Morante Group.' Daniele knew that Franco had disapproved of Marcello's decision, and now he wondered if Marcello had suspected the other man might try to seize control of the company. 'In the next few days, I will bring Paloma to Livorno so that she can make a statement to the press.'

'I am Paloma's only living relative apart from her mother and I would like to offer her my condolences if you will tell me where she is.' Franco's tone had changed, and he showed no sign of his earlier hostility, but Daniele did not warm to him or trust him.

'I must respect Paloma's desire for privacy.' As he strode out of Franco's office, he was planning to visit every damn yoga retreat in Ireland, in search of the missing heiress.

Daniele's phone rang and he quickly answered it when he saw that Paloma's flatmate, whom he had spoken to earlier, was calling him. 'Laura?'

'Mr Berardo, I lied when I said that Paloma is in Ireland. She works for a charity and is teaching at a school in west Africa. There has been civil unrest and violence in Mali for many years, and Paloma didn't tell her grandfather what she was doing because he would worry about her. As a safety precaution, we set up a code word, and if Paloma ever sent me the code, I was to call you and tell you that she is in Mali.'

Daniele frowned. 'Why did Paloma ask you to call *me*?'

'She said that her grandfather trusts you implicitly and she has faith in his judgement.' The urgency in the young woman's voice sent a ripple of unease through Daniele. 'A few minutes ago, I received a text from Paloma and it's the code word. I'm worried that she is in some kind of trouble.'

CHAPTER ONE

PALOMA PEERED THROUGH the tiny window in the hut. All she could see outside was dusty desert, a few scrubby trees and the glint of the gun, slung across the shoulder of one of her captors, who was guarding the compound.

The adrenaline that had pumped through her when two masked gunmen had burst into the school where she had been teaching a class of young Malian girls had helped her to remain calm when she'd been bundled into a truck and driven away. But the hours she'd spent locked in the stifling hut, with barely enough food or water, were taking their toll and she felt scared and helpless.

At least she had managed to send a text to alert her flatmate in London before one of the gunmen had seized her phone. Laura should have contacted Daniele Berardo by now. But realistically, how could a computer geek help her in her present situation? Paloma thought bleakly. Not that there was anything remotely geeky about Daniele, she acknowledged. With his stunning good looks and potent sex appeal, he could be a film star rather than an IT expert and owner of the biggest tech company in Italy.

Her stomach muscles clenched as she visualised Daniele. The press had labelled the self-made multimillionaire Italy's most eligible bachelor, and his handsome face with a faintly sardonic expression appeared regularly in the gossip pages. Invariably he was photographed with a different beautiful woman on his arm. Paloma had spent more time than she was comfortable admitting searching for Daniele on social media sites. The last time she had actually seen him in the flesh had been three years ago.

Despite the intense heat inside her prison, Paloma shuddered as she recalled the most humiliating moments of her life. When Daniele had asked her to dance at a ball hosted by her grandfather, she should have realised that he was simply being polite. She'd had a massive crush on Daniele since she was a teenager, and the champagne she'd drunk during the evening had made her feel daring and encouraged her to press herself up close to his whipcord body when he'd placed his hands on her waist while they danced.

His terse comment that she needed some fresh air as he'd escorted her out of the ballroom had not burst her romantic bubble. They had been alone in the garden and Paloma had curved her arms around his neck and tugged his face towards her so that she could press her lips against his.

Daniele had stiffened, and his hands had gripped her arms as if he'd meant to pull them down. His mouth had been hard and unyielding, like the man himself. But then he'd made a harsh sound in his throat that had sent a coil of heat through Paloma as Daniele had taken control of the kiss. His lips had moved over hers with devastating mastery as he'd explored her mouth and owned it, owned her.

She had held nothing back, and the intensity of her passion had shocked her. But even more shocking had been when Daniele had suddenly wrenched his mouth from hers and set her away from him.

'That should not have happened,' he'd said in a cold voice that had stung her like the lash of a whip. 'Your grandfather would expect a better standard of behaviour from both of us. I suggest we forget that this regrettable incident ever took place.'

Burning up with embarrassment, Paloma had fled back to the house, and she'd left Italy the next day without seeing Daniele again. For the past three years, she had only visited her grandfather when she'd been certain that Daniele would not be in Livorno. Even her decision to marry Calum barely a month after their first date had, in hindsight, been partly to prove that she was over her infatuation with Daniele.

But Marcello had made no secret of the high esteem in which he held Daniele. Paloma hoped he would try to help her because of the affection he felt for her grandfather. Guilt tugged on her fraught emotions as she imagined how worried Nonno would be if he learned that she had been snatched by armed men. One reason for her decision to come to Africa on a volunteer scheme had been the admiration she felt for him. Marcello was a renowned philanthropist and he had established the Morante Foundation, which supported charity projects in Italy and around the world, funded by a percentage of the profits from his business, Morante Group.

Paloma had grown up knowing that she would inherit the company one day. When her father, Marcello's only son, had died in a tragic accident, her destiny had been assured. But her grandfather was likely to remain in charge of Morante Group for many more years, and Paloma had wanted to make her own way in the world, and experience different aspects of life, before she took on the responsibility of heading the company. She had become a fundraising manager for a children's charity, supporting communities in Africa. But spending every day in a comfortable office had felt distant from the problems in Mali, where there was widespread poverty and a lack of education, and she had seized the chance to teach at the school where she could make a real difference to the lives of her pupils.

What was going to happen to her? Paloma wondered fearfully. She'd hardly slept since she had been snatched and she was exhausted. Her head drooped down until her chin rested on her chest. She must have dozed, and woke with a start to the sound of a vehicle racing across the compound, and the terrifying noise of gunfire. Immediately her heart began to thump, and she jumped to her feet just as the door of the hut was flung open.

A figure dressed in khaki-coloured combat clothes and a balaclava covering his face, with two narrow slits cut out over his eyes, stood in the doorway. The man—Paloma guessed from his height and powerful build that he was male—was not one of the kidnappers who had taken her from the school. But his manner was authoritative, and she guessed he could be their leader. He was armed with an assault rifle and she instinctively backed away from him.

'Come with me,' he growled.

She must have imagined that he sounded vaguely familiar. Fearfully, Paloma backed away from him. 'Who are you?' Her voice shook as she heard the *pop-pop* of gunfire outside the hut.

Without another word, the man lurched towards her, scooped her off her feet and slung her over his shoulder. It happened so fast that Paloma did not have time to struggle. He carried her out of the hut, and she heard rough male voices. Once again, she had a sense of familiarity, but her brain had frozen, and she could not understand what was being said.

There was the sound of an engine revving, and then she was thrown into the back of a truck and her head hit the metal floor with a *thunk*. She attempted to sit up, but her captor leapt into the truck, slammed the door shut and flung himself on top of her as the vehicle was driven off at speed.

'Get off me!' Paloma braced her hands on the man's chest and attempted to push him away, but it was like trying to shift a granite boulder. She had trained in martial arts for years, but the reality of trying to defend herself against someone who was so much bigger and stronger than her was impossible. The knowledge that she was at her captor's mercy fired her temper. 'Pick on someone your own size, you *jerk*. Do you get a thrill from overpowering a defenceless woman and children?'

She remembered the terror on the faces of her pupils when the gunmen had burst into the classroom. 'What have you done with the girls from the school? Let them go,' she pleaded.

'Their families can't afford to pay a ransom. I am more valuable to you than a group of school-girls. My grandfather is a rich man, and he will pay for my release, but only if you allow the girls to go free.'

She glared into the man's eyes that were the only part of his face not covered by his bala-clava. Eyes the golden-brown colour of sherry glittered back at her. Paloma became aware of his hard thighs pressed against her, and beneath her hands, she felt the definition of an impres-sive six-pack through his shirt.

Unbelievably she felt a flutter of awareness in the pit of her stomach. Not just awareness, but familiarity. Her subconscious mind recog-nised the impressive musculature of the male body stretched out on top of her, and her senses stirred when she breathed in the evocative scent of his aftershave. Only one man had ever elic-ited such an intense response in her.

She must be hallucinating, Paloma decided. Her captor couldn't be… She grabbed the edge of the man's balaclava and tore it off his face. Her eyes widened in shock. *'Daniele!'*

'Ciao, cara,' he drawled in his sexy, accented voice that made her toes curl inside her trainers.

When Daniele had carried her out of the hut, he must have spoken in Italian to the driver of the truck. Paloma spoke Italian fluently, but

English was her first language, and she'd been unable to think straight in the tense situation.

She gasped when she heard a metallic thud on the side of the truck.

'Vai più veloce!' Daniele told the driver urgently.

Paloma knew he had told him to go faster. Fear cramped in her stomach when she realised that the thudding sound was bullets striking the metal truck. They were being chased by the other gunmen who were shooting at them.

She stared up at Daniele and it occurred to her that he was lying on top of her to protect her with his body if a bullet came through the window. The gleam in his eyes caused her heart to miss a beat.

'I don't understand,' she said shakily. 'You're a computer geek.' She had only ever seen him at Morante Group's offices or at her grandfather's opulent palazzo. Daniele had always worn a designer suit and been impeccably groomed. Now he reminded her of a pirate with his black hair falling across his brow and thick stubble covering his jaw.

'I did not realise that you had such an unflattering opinion of me,' he said drily.

His face was so close to hers that Paloma felt his breath graze her cheek. She could not look away from his sensual mouth as memories flooded her mind of being expertly kissed by him. The weight of his body held her pinned to the floor of the truck, and a purely feminine instinct made her splay her thighs a little so that her pelvis was flush with his.

His jaw clenched, and he flexed his arms and abruptly pushed himself off her. 'Stay where you are,' he ordered before he rolled across to the side of the truck, aimed his rifle out of the window and fired several rounds. *'Evvai!'* There was satisfaction in his voice. 'It's safe for you to sit up,' he told Paloma. 'I shot out a front tyre on the other truck. The men who kidnapped you can't harm you now.'

'Who *are* you?' she muttered.

'I trained as a soldier in the Italian Army and belonged to the Ninth Paratroopers Assault Regiment. The regiment is a special forces unit, like the SAS in the British Army.' There was quiet pride in Daniele's voice. 'An injury I sustained while I was on active service put an end to my military career, but I kept in touch with some of the other paras. When your flatmate told me you were in trouble, I contacted the school in Mali and learned that you had been kidnapped.' His mouth tightened. 'The country is notoriously dangerous, and kidnapping, especially of foreigners, is a serious threat. It was irresponsible of you to come here.'

'I was aware of the risks,' Paloma muttered. 'But there is a shortage of schools and teachers in Mali, and without access to education, children's life chances are reduced. Teaching was a practical way that I could help.' She pushed her hair out of her eyes, certain she must look a bedraggled, sweaty mess. Reaction to her ordeal was setting in, and the censure in Daniele's voice added guilt to the mix of her emotions. 'I didn't expect you would put your life in danger to rescue me. Thank you.' She flushed as she acknowledged how inadequate her words were.

'I promised your grandfather I would protect you,' Daniele said curtly. Instantly Paloma felt that she was a liability. She had sometimes felt stifled by Nonno's overprotectiveness. 'I was assisted by some of my old army friends,' Daniele told her. 'We had a tip-off that led us to where the gunmen were holding you and I planned a rescue mission. In a few minutes we will arrive at an airstrip where a plane is waiting to fly us out of here.'

'Does my grandfather know what happened to me?'

'No.' Daniele turned his head away and stared out of the window. Paloma had the feeling that he was avoiding her gaze.

'Thank you for keeping my kidnap ordeal from Nonno,' she said huskily. 'I had made up a story that I was spending time at a wellness retreat because I didn't want him to worry about me.'

'There is something I must tell you.' Daniele swore when the truck jolted on the uneven ground and Paloma fell against him. She put her hands on the solid wall of his chest to steady herself and was aware that his gaze had dropped to where her sweat-damp T-shirt was clinging to her breasts. To her horror, she felt her nipples harden, and she quickly shifted away from him. 'I'll talk to you when we are on the plane,' Daniele said roughly.

A sense of dread dropped into the pit of Paloma's stomach at his serious tone. They had reached an airfield and the truck pulled up next to a plane. She put her hand on Daniele's arm. 'Talk to me now.'

He exhaled slowly. 'There is no easy way to break the news to you, *cara*. Marcello is dead.'

Her heart stopped. 'It's not true. It can't be.' She searched Daniele's face for reassurance that she had misunderstood him but found none. 'Nonno is not a young man, but he is remarkably fit and healthy for his age.' It *had* to be a mistake. Paloma could not accept what Daniele had told her.

'I'm sorry. I realise what a shock this is for you. Your grandfather had an aortic aneurysm. In layman's terms, it means that the main blood vessel from his heart ruptured. We were playing golf when he collapsed with chest pains. I immediately called the emergency services and the medics fought to save him, but he died before he reached the hospital.'

'Were you with him when…when he died?' Paloma choked. Her throat was clogged with tears as the terrible truth sank in that she would never see her beloved Nonno again.

'I was,' Daniele assured her.

'I'm glad he wasn't alone.' Guilt felt like a knife through her heart. She should have been with her grandfather. He had tried to persuade her to move to Italy and become his assistant at Morante Group to prepare for the role that would one day be hers. She'd assumed that she had plenty of time to spread her wings first. Paloma swallowed a sob. 'When did Nonno collapse?'

'Two days ago. I've managed to keep a news blackout and only a handful of people know about Marcello's death.' Daniele hesitated. 'It is possible that someone on Morante Group's board of trustees arranged for you to disappear.'

Paloma stared at him. 'Why would any of them do that?'

'You are the sole heiress to your grandfather's fortune,' Daniele reminded her. 'The money comes to you straight away, and when you are twenty-five, you will take control of the company, as Marcello decreed in his will. But if something should happen to you, half of your inheritance is to be paid to the Morante Foundation charity and the other half will be divided equally between the eight board members, including your great-uncle Franco, but not myself. Your grandfather gave me a lifelong position on the board, but I am not a beneficiary of his will. In the event of your death, the other trustees stand to become multimillionaires, and the board will decide who to appoint as the new head of Morante Group.'

'I'm young and healthy, and nothing is likely to happen to me.' Paloma bit her lip when Daniele rolled his eyes. 'You said yourself that kidnapping of foreigners is common in Mali.'

'I suppose it *could* be a coincidence that you were seized soon after Marcello died, but in my experience, coincidences are rare,' Daniele said cynically. 'If your flatmate hadn't alerted me, I would not have known where to look for you. But someone knew the Morante heiress was in Mali, and I believe that person hoped to prevent you from claiming your inheritance.'

CHAPTER TWO

DANIELE RAPPED ON the bedroom door but got no response. He tried the handle but was not surprised to find that the door was locked. The previous evening, he had brought Paloma to a hotel owned by his close friend whom he trusted implicitly. In the penthouse suite, Paloma had locked herself in one of the bedrooms and Daniele had heard her crying for hours.

He had paced up and down the corridor outside her room, wondering if he should offer to try to comfort her as he had done after her father had been killed in a speedboat accident eight years ago. Paloma had been sixteen and still a child in Daniele's eyes. A rapport had grown between them when he'd shared his experience of losing his own father when he had been a teenager.

But Paloma was no longer a schoolgirl, a fact that Daniele had been all too aware of when he'd flung himself on top of her in the back of the truck to protect her from the bullets that the kidnappers had been firing indiscriminately. His jaw clenched as he remembered how his body had reacted to the feel of Paloma's soft curves beneath him. He had been shocked, frankly, by the kick of awareness in the pit of his stomach.

At thirty-six, he was way past the age of behaving like a hormonal adolescent. He dated selectively and enjoyed women's company both in and out of the bedroom, although he had never felt an inclination to marry. It said a lot about him, Daniele acknowledged. He had guarded his emotions since he'd been five years old and watched his mother drive away from the family home. She had promised to visit him often, but she'd never come back. Eventually Daniele had given up staring out of the window in the hope of seeing her car turn the corner of the road. It had been an early lesson that promises were easily made and just as easily broken. A few years later, he had been invited to visit his mother, who had remarried, and he'd met his little half-brother. But since then, Daniele had not had any further contact with that side of his family for twenty-seven years.

He pulled his thoughts from the past and knocked on the door again. 'Paloma, you need to eat. I've arranged for dinner to be served here in the suite.'

'I'm not hungry.' Her voice was muffled. 'I want to be alone.'

Daniele frowned. He had given Paloma's grandfather his word that he would take care of her, which meant he must help her to secure her place as the head of Morante Group.

'You are not the only one who is devastated by Marcello's death,' he said gruffly. 'I share your grief. But you are your grandfather's successor, and he would want you to show strong leadership of the company. I ordered some clothes for you from the hotel's boutique. I'll leave them outside the door.' His words were met with silence. 'There are things we need to discuss, and I do not intend to talk to you through the door. Don't make me break it down.'

'You wouldn't dare.'

'I never make idle threats, *cara*.' Daniele walked back to the sitting room, cursing as his leg throbbed. The old injury was a permanent reminder of the events that had led to him meeting Marcello Morante. Ten years ago, he had paid a heavy price for saving Marcello's life, but Marcello had in turn saved Daniele from the dark place he'd fallen into and given him the chance of a glittering future.

The grief that Daniele had suppressed since his old friend's death felt like a knife blade through his heart. He took a bottle of beer from the fridge and opened it before he stepped out onto the balcony. Now that Paloma was safe, he could finally focus on the man who had meant so much to him.

With his last breaths, Marcello had told Daniele that he'd thought of him as a grandson. It was ironic, Daniele brooded, that his real grandfather, who had disowned him when he was a child, had died only days before Marcello. Daniele had not mourned his mother's father, and in fact, he'd only met the Conte Alfonso Farnesi on one humiliating occasion when he had been made to feel that he was muck on the sole of his grandfather's shoe.

Daniele had been nine when his mother had unexpectedly invited him to the Farnesi estate near Florence. She had not been in contact since she'd left four years earlier and she'd divorced Daniele's father and remarried. There had been photos in the newspapers of her and her new husband, who was from an aristocratic banking family. Some while later, it had been reported that she had given birth to a son by her second husband.

Daniele had been desperate to see his mother and excited to meet his half-brother, Stefano. But the visit had gone badly. He'd felt awkward when he'd walked into his grandfather Alfonso's imposing villa where his mother and her new family lived. On the walls were paintings of grand-looking men and women. The House of Farnesi had been an important family since the time of the Renaissance. But it had been made clear to Daniele that his portrait would never hang alongside his glorious ancestors. His father was a common soldier, and his grandfather was determined that the Farnesi blue-blooded lineage would not be tainted by a low-born grandson.

Under ancient nobility laws, titles were passed down through the male line. But if, as in Conte Farnesi's case, he had a daughter, but no son, the title could skip a generation and be passed to the first male grandchild. By rights, that should have been Daniele. But during that infamous visit, Alfonso had announced that he'd disinherited Daniele and made Stefano his heir.

Daniele forced his mind away from bitter memories of his childhood and took a long swig of beer. The title of Conte was only a courtesy, as official recognition of Italian nobility had ended decades ago. He'd assumed that he had come to terms with being overlooked by his grandfather and rejected by his mother. But before he'd left Italy for Africa, the newspapers had been full of reports of the death of the seventeenth Conte Farnesi. Much gushing prose had been printed about Alfonso's successor, his grandson Stefano, who would take the surname Farnesi.

Daniele had studied the newspaper photo of his mother looking proudly at his half-brother

and he'd been surprised at how much it still rankled that he was not good enough for her. He had
made a fortune by using his brain and working
hard, and his online affiliate marketing company, Premio, was ranked in the top ten most
successful businesses in Italy. But despite his
achievements, his mother would never be proud
of him because his father had not belonged to
the nobility.

Daniele heard footsteps behind him. He
turned around and inhaled sharply as he watched
Paloma walk towards him. During her kidnap
ordeal, she had worn the same T-shirt and shorts
for days, but despite looking tired and dishev-
elled, she had still been beautiful when Daniele
had rescued her from her captors.

This evening she was utterly breathtaking.
The clothes that had been delivered from the
hotel's boutique were typical holiday wear.
Paloma was dressed in a long, kaftan-style gar-
ment made of fine white cotton, with delicate
gold embroidery along the V-shaped neckline.
A wide belt of the same material emphasised
her tiny waist. As she walked, the side splits
on either side of the skirt parted to reveal her
slim legs.

Daniele heard the thunder of his pulse in his
ears and was conscious that his blood had surged
down to his groin. The kick of awareness was
even stronger than he'd felt in the truck when he

had stretched his body out on top of Paloma to shield her from the gunmen's bullets. He could not tear his gaze from her long, chestnut-brown hair that fell midway to her waist and gleamed like raw silk in the light from the lamps on the balcony. The lemony scent of shampoo, mingled with the subtle, floral fragrance of her perfume, assailed his senses and his pulse quickened.

He was struck by the realisation that the pretty teenager he had first met nearly a decade ago, and even the naive but achingly lovely twenty-one-year-old intern Paloma had been three years ago, had not prepared him for the exquisite and sensuous woman who halted in front of him.

Her dark eyelashes swept upwards and eyes the intense blue of lapis lazuli glared at him. 'You always were as cold as a block of ice, Daniele.'

He was fascinated and relieved to see the pink flush that highlighted Paloma's delicate cheekbones. Her face had been ashen when he'd half carried her into the hotel, but now the evidence of her temper was a good sign. She would need to be strong. Marcello was a hard act to follow, and Daniele did not know if Paloma was up to the task, but it was his duty to give her the chance to find out.

'I have lost my grandfather, who I loved more than anyone in the world.' Her voice shook. 'Would it hurt you to show a little compassion?'

Daniele's eyes dropped to her lips, which trembled slightly before she pressed them together. He sensed she was struggling to control her emotions, and he was furious with himself for imagining covering her lush mouth with his. Paloma was out of bounds, and the quicker his libido accepted that fact, the better. He wondered what she would say if he admitted that, far from being a block of ice, he was on fire. Fortunately, he was a master at concealing his thoughts behind an enigmatic expression.

'I gave you the space that I thought you needed, but time is against us,' he told her. 'You must be at Morante Group's offices tomorrow to make a formal announcement of Marcello's death. We will fly to Italy on a private jet first thing in the morning.'

She frowned. 'You mean we are not in Italy? I'd assumed it was where we were headed when we left Mali, but I was thinking about Nonno, and I didn't take much notice of anything else.' Paloma stepped closer to the balcony rail and looked out. Night had fallen, and the moon was a huge silver ball reflected in the pool below. 'I can see palm trees. Where are we?'

'Tunisia. A friend of mine, Enrique, owns the hotel. Another ex-army friend piloted the plane that was used in the operation to rescue you. I decided against taking you to Italy until I'd had a chance to try and find out who was behind the kidnap plot. For your safety, only Enrique knows that you are staying here.'

'You have useful friends,' Paloma murmured wryly. She slanted Daniele a look when he came to stand beside her. 'I keep hoping that I will wake up and find it was all a dream. Being kidnapped, and then you turning up to rescue me.' She swallowed. 'Nonno dying. It all seems unreal. I can't believe that the two events are linked. The political situation in Mali is unstable and militia groups have a history of attacking civilians.'

'The gunmen who snatched you from the school were not Malian nationals.'

'How do you know?'

'A couple of my guys stayed behind in Mali to carry out surveillance. The gunmen were picked up by the police but refused to say who they were working for.' Daniele exhaled heavily. Paloma needed to understand the seriousness of the situation. 'The kidnappers escaped from custody, or, more likely, someone was paid to allow them to go free. Who was behind the plot to kidnap you? That's what I'd like to know.'

'I don't believe anyone on the board of trustees could be involved. They are…' she bit her lip '…were Nonno's friends and I have known them all my life.'

Daniele shrugged. 'At least two of them have financial problems that would be resolved if you were not around and your grandfather's fortune was split between the board members.'

'It's always about money,' Paloma burst out. 'People believe that wealth brings happiness, but not in my experience. I'm convinced that my family is cursed. Nonno adored his wife, but my grandmother died giving birth to my father. Papa was only forty when he was killed in a speedboat race. Now my grandfather has gone too, and you say that my safety is threatened because I am a rich heiress. Sometimes I wish I could walk away from it all,' she muttered.

Daniele tore his gaze from Paloma's breasts rising and falling swiftly beneath her dress, and silently cursed his damnable attraction to her that he was determined to resist. 'If I don't get you to Livorno by tomorrow, your wish may come true.'

'What do you mean?'

A knock on the door of the suite gave him the excuse to shelve the conversation for a while. 'That will be dinner,' he said as he ushered Paloma inside and held out a chair for her to be seated at the table. A waiter came in, pushing a trolley laden with dishes. Once the food had been served, the wine poured and the candles on the table lit, the waiter left them alone.

Daniele was relieved when Paloma picked up her fork and started to eat some couscous and roasted vegetables. She looked fragile, and he found himself wanting to comfort her, hold her. His jaw clenched as his body responded to the idea of taking her into his arms so that her small breasts were crushed against his chest. Marcello had asked him to protect Paloma, and Daniele was determined to honour his friend's last request.

'I noticed you were limping just now,' she commented. 'Have you hurt your leg?'

'I was shot…'

Paloma dropped her fork and it clattered against the china plate. 'You mean you were hit by a bullet when the gunmen were firing at us! Why didn't you tell me? It's my fault you are injured.'

'It's an old injury,' Daniele quickly assured her. 'It happened years ago when I was in the army. My kneecap was shattered, and I had several rounds of surgery to rebuild it. Most of the time it's fine, but I landed heavily on my knee when we jumped into the truck to get away from the kidnappers.'

'Was your injury the reason you left the army?'

'Yes, unfortunately.' He looked across the table and saw Paloma's eyes widen at his curt reply. 'The army was my life. I had wanted to join up since I was a kid, to honour my father.'

'I remember you told me that your father died while he was a soldier, serving in Bosnia.'

'He was part of the peace-keeping force and was killed by a sniper.'

'So you became a soldier like your dad. What happened to you?'

'One of my missions in the special forces was to work undercover. I was sent to infiltrate a Mafia gang who were responsible for several high-profile kidnappings and murders. I discovered that Marcello Morante was the gang's next target and managed to alert the authorities in time to foil the plot. Your grandfather was safe, but my cover had been blown, and the Mafia boss ordered my execution.'

Daniele hesitated when Paloma gasped. Nausea churned in his stomach as memories flooded back. Counselling had helped him to process what had happened, but he would never forget the sickening terror he'd felt when the gang had discovered his identity, and he'd been certain he was going to die.

'I was driven to a remote field and shot,' he explained unemotionally. 'The injury was deliberately not immediately fatal so that I would slowly bleed to death.'

'Oh, Daniele.' Paloma's soft voice tugged on something buried deep inside him. An unexpected longing for tenderness that he quickly dismissed. In his heart he would always be a soldier, and perhaps a part of him would always be the boy who had watched his mother leave. 'How did you survive?' Paloma asked.

'I managed to crawl across the field after the assassins had driven away.' For years afterwards, his nightmares had dragged him back to the darkness and the agonising pain of his shattered knee as blood had poured from the bullet wound. 'I came to a farmer's track, and by a million-to-one chance, some tourists were lost and had stopped to look at the map. They patched me up and drove me to the nearest hospital. If they had found me five minutes later, it would have been too late, and I would have bled out.'

'I had no idea that you nearly lost your life to keep my grandfather safe. It explains the bond that existed between you and Nonno.'

Daniele shrugged. 'I was doing my job. I didn't know Marcello then. But he found out that I had prevented him from being kidnapped, and he came to see me. I had just learned that, despite numerous operations, my knee was permanently damaged, and my army career was over. I was twenty-six and felt like my life was over.'

He grimaced. 'Marcello offered to pay me compensation, but I was a surly devil and told him what he could do with his money. I didn't want handouts, and I was determined to make my own fortune. I had always been interested in computers and programming, and while I'd been in hospital for months, I'd developed a smart payment app for mobile phones. Remember, this was ten years ago, and the idea was innovative. Marcello agreed to invest in my start-up company. It was an instant success, and three years later, I became a millionaire when I sold the business. Your grandfather persuaded me to join Morante Group as an IT consultant, and I established an online marketing presence that helped to make the company a global brand.'

'Nonno said you dragged Morante Group into the twenty-first century,' Paloma murmured. 'I know he admired you.'

'I was honoured to have had your grandfather as my friend. He was a great man. But the same cannot be said about Franco Zambrotta.'

Paloma had finished eating, and she took a sip of wine before setting her glass down on the table. 'What have you got against Uncle Franco?'

The red wine had stained her lips. Daniele's gaze lingered on her lush mouth and he wondered if she tasted as intoxicating as she had three years ago. He would never find out, he resolved grimly. Marcello had made him responsible for Paloma, and in the past twenty-four hours, Daniele had formed a crazy plan that would allow him to keep her safe and protect her position at Morante Group. But he could not let his inconvenient desire for her undermine his self-control.

'Your great-uncle intends to call for a vote of no confidence in you,' he said abruptly. 'If he gains the support of the majority of the board of trustees, you will effectively be fired, or at least sidelined, and Franco will put himself up as joint chairman and CEO of Morante Group.'

Paloma's eyes widened. 'He can't do that, can he?'

'I'm afraid he can. If he is voted in as the new head of the company, he intends to reduce the annual donation to the Morante Foundation. You probably know that your grandfather insisted on forty per cent of the business's profits being paid to the charity.'

'A policy that I am determined will continue. I can't believe the other board members would agree to pay less of the profits to the charitable foundation that was so important to Nonno.'

'They might if Franco offers a financial sweetener to the trustees. Legally he could pay them bonus dividends during financial restructuring of the company. But in order for that to happen, the board would first have to replace you with Franco. Under the terms of Marcello's will, Franco will be the acting head of Morante Group until your twenty-fifth birthday. That's in December, isn't it?' When Paloma nodded, Daniele continued, 'Franco will have eight months to win the support of the board.'

'If my grandfather had wanted Uncle Franco

to succeed him, instead of me, he would have altered his will. The fact that he didn't must mean that he had faith in my ability to run the company. Surely the board will abide by Marcello's wishes?'

Daniele sighed. 'You are an unknown quantity. Perhaps if you had moved to Italy when you finished university and worked at the company as Marcello had hoped, you would not have been seen as an outsider.'

'I'm not completely clueless. I have a master's degree in business. However, I realise that I lack the necessary experience to run Morante Group. I'd expected Nonno to be around for years to advise me.' Paloma's voice wobbled. 'Now I find myself responsible for the business that my grandfather started before I was born. He was both chairman and CEO, but I'm thinking of splitting the roles and appointing a CEO who will lead the executive management team.'

'I suppose that might allay some of the board's concerns. But there is still the matter of your marriage.'

Paloma flushed. 'My marriage was a mistake. I don't understand why it should matter to anyone else, especially as I am now divorced.'

'I heard it was an expensive mistake because you had not asked your husband to sign a prenuptial agreement before the wedding,' Daniele said drily. He told himself it was a coincidence that the last time he'd got extremely drunk had been the night he'd learned of Paloma's surprise marriage. 'Franco has made the point that if you succeed your grandfather and were to rush into another marriage, your new spouse could be entitled to half of Morante Group's assets in a divorce settlement.'

Paloma's long lashes swept down to hide her expression. 'There is a saying—once bitten, twice shy,' she said curtly. 'I have no intention of marrying again.'

'That's a pity,' Daniele drawled, 'because I strongly advise you to marry me.'

CHAPTER THREE

'VERY FUNNY,' PALOMA MUTTERED. Inside, she was cringing with embarrassment at Daniele's mention of her marriage that had lasted barely long enough for the ink to dry on the register. Worse still, it had been Daniele's rejection that had sent her rushing back to England instead of relocating to Italy as her grandfather had wanted her to do. She'd met Calum soon after her return to London and been flattered by his attention.

Paloma pushed away uncomfortable memories of her ex-husband and forced herself to look at Daniele. 'This is not the time for jokes.'

'It wasn't a joke. I am making a serious proposition.' He held her gaze, and in the glow of the candlelight, his eyes were the golden colour of amber. Lion's eyes, Paloma thought. Daniele reminded her of a predatory big cat. He gave the impression of being relaxed as he leaned back in his chair, but there was something intrinsically powerful about him, and his eyes gleaming beneath his thick black lashes were watchful and alert.

He was unfairly gorgeous, in faded jeans and a cream shirt, unbuttoned at the neck to reveal a sprinkling of black chest hairs. His shirtsleeves were rolled up to the elbows, showing his darkly tanned forearms and the glint of a discreetly expensive-looking gold watch on his wrist. Paloma was aware of a melting sensation in the pit of her stomach that only Daniele had ever induced. He must be about thirty-six now, but there were no silver strands in his raven's-wing dark hair. She fancied that his face was leaner, harder, the sharp cheekbones more defined. His mouth was perfection and offered the same sensual invitation that had led her to behave uncharacteristically recklessly three years ago.

It was a good thing she had got over her juvenile crush on him, Paloma assured herself. 'Explain yourself, Daniele,' she demanded. 'The last time we met, it was obvious you couldn't bear to touch me. I don't flatter myself that you actually *want* to marry me.'

He looked startled for a moment before his features became unreadable again. 'I have racked my brains to find another way that I can protect you and your interests with Morante Group as I promised your grandfather I would do. A temporary marriage until you are twenty-five is the best solution I can come up with.'

'I don't need your protection,' Paloma said stiffly. She understood that Daniele was acting out of the deep loyalty he felt for her grandfather, but her pride was stung by his obvious reluctance to have any sort of involvement with her. 'Being kidnapped was the most terrifying ordeal I have ever experienced,' she admitted. 'But I don't buy into your conspiracy theory that someone on the board of trustees wants me out of the way.'

'Setting aside the question of who was behind the kidnap plot, Franco Zambrotta is serious about seizing control of the company. I have heard from a private source that he is gaining support from more board members.'

'How would it help me if I married you?' It was out of the question. Nothing would persuade Paloma to agree to Daniele's astonishing proposition, but she was curious to know the reason behind it.

'Marcello made me vice president of the board, and I am popular with most of the trustees, with the exception of Franco and one or two of his close cronies. I believe the majority of the board will approve of our marriage for two reasons. Firstly, I have the business experience that you lack, and I can prepare you for when you take control of the company. Secondly, if you are my wife, there will be no chance of you marrying without a prenuptial agreement in place to safeguard Morante Group's assets.'

'Are you saying you would be willing to sign a prenup?'

'Certainly. In fact, I'd insist on it. A legal agreement would be drawn up to protect the entirety of your inheritance and the company's assets. I already own a highly successful business and I am wealthy. I don't want your money or your company, *cara*.'

'You must want something from me. Everyone always does,' Paloma said flatly. Ever since she had been old enough to understand that she was an heiress to a vast fortune, she had felt set apart from her peers and wary of people's motives for wanting to be her friend.

Across the table, Daniele gave her a speculative look. 'I don't deny it would be advantageous for me to marry the granddaughter of a marchese. You were born into one of the oldest Italian noble families and your heritage gives you a certain status in society that I, as an entrepreneur who made my fortune through hard work and innovation, can never attain.'

'And that matters to you?'

'It matters to my mother,' Daniele said in a grim voice. 'Her aristocratic family disapproved of her marriage to my father because he had no title and was, in their opinion, a common soldier. My grandfather threatened to cut my mother out of his will unless she divorced my father and cut all ties with me, which she did.'

Paloma stared at Daniele. Her parents had divorced acrimoniously when she was a child, and her mother had been awarded custody, but she'd seen her father fairly regularly. The break-up had been a painful time. How much worse it must have been for Daniele when his mother had cut him out of her life. 'How old were you when she went away?'

'Five. My father brought me up, but he was often sent away on military postings, and I spent a lot of time with my grandmother. When my father was killed, I lived with my grandmother because my mother refused to take me back. She'd remarried and had another son. My half-brother recently became the new Conte Farnesi following my grandfather's death.'

Paloma took a deep breath. 'So you would be willing to marry me to impress your mother with an aristocratic bride?' It was stupid to feel so hurt, she told herself. Daniele was no different from everyone else who valued her for her financial worth or, in his case, her pedigree.

'The marriage would be advantageous to both of us. I would help you to secure your position as head of Morante Group,' he reminded her.

Paloma leapt to her feet. She needed to get away from Daniele before her emotions overwhelmed her. 'If necessary, I'll sign a statement saying that I will not marry anyone without the approval of the board of trustees.' It took all her effort to keep her voice steady, but she was damned if she'd let Daniele see how humiliated she felt. 'I know that my grandfather had the best intentions.' She blinked away tears as she thought of Nonno, the only person who had truly loved her. 'But to him I was always a little girl. I'm not. I am an adult, and I don't need your help or protection.'

She marched across the room and paused in the doorway, turning her head to give Daniele a fulminating glare. 'You will have to find yourself another aristocratic bride. If we were the last two people on the planet, I still wouldn't marry you.'

The pool had been warm when Paloma had started swimming. She'd powered through the water, completing lap after lap while she focused on her breathing to block out her chaotic thoughts. Now, though, she was tired, and the water felt chilly. There had been several other hotel guests swimming or sitting on the poolside when she'd arrived. But when she looked around, she discovered that they had gone, and she was alone.

The pool area was surrounded by trees and shrubs, and the darkness preyed on Paloma's imagination. Was Daniele right, and the men who had seized her in Mali were working for some unknown person who wanted to prevent her from claiming her inheritance? *Be logical,* she told herself sternly. Daniele had said that no one knew she was staying at the hotel in Tunisia. There were not hordes of kidnappers lurking in the shadows.

All the same, she wished she'd told him she was going to the pool. After dinner she had fled to her room, reeling from his shocking marriage proposition. But she'd felt restless and had decided to go for a swim. There had been a swimsuit among the clothes that Daniele had ordered from the hotel's boutique. Paloma had heard him talking on his phone when she'd slipped out of the suite.

Her teeth were chattering when she swam to the edge of the pool. But as she was about to climb up the steps, she heard a rustling noise from the bushes, and she froze. The memory of the terrifying moment when the gunmen had burst into the classroom in Mali stretched her overwrought emotions to breaking point. Was someone aiming a gun at her, his finger on the trigger as he waited for her to climb out of the pool? The leaves on the bushes shook, even though there was no breeze. Heart pounding in her chest, Paloma opened her mouth and screamed.

Immediately she heard footsteps running

across the terrace and saw Daniele's reassuringly big and powerful figure charging towards the pool. He halted next to the steps and his eyes glittered in the darkness. 'What happened? Are you hurt?'

'There's someone in the bushes over there.' She was shivering so badly with a mixture of cold and fear that she could barely get the words out. The story Daniele had told her of how he had foiled a Mafia plot to kidnap her grandfather had stuck in her mind. Nonno's death meant that she was now incredibly rich and a target for criminals who might try to snatch her and demand a ransom for her release. 'Be careful,' she urged Daniele in a shaky whisper as he strode towards the shadowy area at the edge of the terrace.

'Who is there?' he demanded. Paloma held her breath when there was more movement from the bushes. Daniele let out a low laugh as a cat leapt out and landed on its four paws on the tiles. 'There's your culprit. Stray cats are a problem around the hotel complex.' The cat gave them a disdainful look and stalked away indignantly.

Relief surged through Paloma. Her emotions were on a knife-edge and something inside her cracked. She climbed out of the pool and buried her face in her hands as sobs shook her slender frame. Once again, Daniele had put himself in potential danger to protect her. He hadn't known that it was a cat, not a gunman, concealed in the bushes. Daniele was the only person she could trust, and she did not resist when he placed his arm across her shoulders and drew her against his muscular body.

'*Va bene, cara,*' he murmured. 'You are safe.'

She felt safe with him. Paloma made a choked sound of protest when Daniele moved away from her, but he returned almost instantly to drape a towel around her shoulders and began to rub her dry.

'Are you feeling warmer?' he asked after a couple of minutes of brisk rubbing.

'A bit.' Her skin was tingling from his ministrations with the towel. She ought to object that he was treating her like a child, but when he pulled her into the circle of his arms once more, she sank against him, feeling the warmth of his body through his shirt transfer to her. He smelled divinely of sandalwood cologne, and she heard the strong thud of his heart beneath her ear when she rested her head on his chest.

'You have been through a lot recently. The events in Mali and the sudden loss of your grandfather. You're in a state of shock.' Daniele's deep voice rumbled through Paloma, and she was soothed by the light touch of his hand as he stroked her hair back from her face.

Nonno was the only person who had made her feel cherished. Her mother led a busy life socialising with her jet-set friends, and as a child Paloma had mostly been left in the care of nannies or sent away to boarding school. Visits to her father had been marred by his jealous mistresses who had resented any attention he had shown his daughter. Paloma had learned to be self-sufficient at a young age, but the truth was she had been lonely all her life. A poor little rich girl was how the tabloids had described her when speculation about the size of the divorce settlement she'd given Calum had made the headlines.

She did not want to think about her ex-husband's cruel deception, or the promises he'd made so glibly but had never intended to keep. She could not bear to think of her darling Nonno, the only person who had valued her for who she was, rather than how much she was worth. Standing in the shelter of Daniele's arms, Paloma closed her eyes and allowed her senses to take over from her conscious thoughts.

The call of the cicadas was a noisy chorus in the still night air, and the fragrance of jasmine growing in pots on the terrace was sweetly sultry. Paloma became aware of a subtle change in Daniele's breathing and felt the quickening of his heartbeat. She was conscious of how much taller than her he was, and of the latent strength of his muscular physique.

In contrast, she felt small and weak like a kitten. Of course she wasn't weak. Her great-uncle Franco and the other board members would discover that she was determined to claim her place at the head of the company she had inherited. But that fight would happen tomorrow. Right now it was bliss to be in Daniele's arms while he threaded his fingers through her long hair.

In a flash, Paloma's dreamy state of relaxation disappeared, replaced with an intense awareness of the man who had featured in every one of her adolescent romantic fantasies. The tiny hairs on her skin prickled and the ache low in her pelvis urged her to press herself closer to Daniele. Her breasts felt heavy, and she wondered if he could feel the hard tips of her nipples through the clingy material of her swimsuit. She tilted her head so that she could look at his face and her heart missed a beat when their eyes met and held. A nerve flickered in his cheek and his dark brows met above his glittering amber gaze.

'Paloma…' There was a warning in his gruff voice, but she could not look away from him or break the connection that throbbed between them. Three years ago, she had made the first move and pressed her lips against his, only for him to spurn her. Now she watched Daniele's dark head descend and her pulse leapt when it seemed that he was about to kiss her. His warm breath whispered over her lips. She could not move, could hardly breathe. Her lashes swept down to hide the longing she was sure he would see in her eyes.

He swore, his voice low and harsh, and abruptly dropped his arms down to his sides so that she swayed on her feet when he stepped back from her. Daniele raked his hand through his hair. 'Go inside. Quickly.' He bit out the command.

Paloma hugged the towel tightly around her. She could not control the tremors that racked her body as reaction to what had happened— or nearly happened—set in. Self-recrimination churned in her stomach. *Idiot!* Why had she stared at Daniele like a lovesick teenager, hoping he would kiss her? He had made it clear that his marriage proposition was so he could fulfil his promise to her grandfather to take care of her. He saw her as his responsibility, nothing more.

He frowned when she did not move. 'For God's sake, go back to the hotel—*now*. And, Paloma,' he said curtly when she turned away from him. 'What just happened. It was nothing. We are both in shock and grieving for Marcello. It's hardly surprising that our emotions are running high.'

Daniele watched Paloma run back to the hotel and was tempted to follow her to make sure she reached the penthouse safely. But he had a more pressing need to discover who had been spying on them. He hadn't imagined the sudden glare of a camera flashbulb from the shadowy area next to the pool. At least it had jolted him to his senses, he thought grimly.

What the hell had he been thinking when he'd pulled Paloma into his arms? But in fairness, when she had broken down and sobbed heartbrokenly, her vulnerability had tugged on something inside him, and his only thought had been to comfort her. He hadn't counted on the fact that Paloma had been a threat to his peace of mind for years. His libido had responded to her softly curvaceous body and her small breasts pressed against his chest. The temptation to kiss her had made him forget the promise he had made her grandfather. Worse, he had momentarily forgotten that Paloma was in danger.

Silently cursing his lack of control, Daniele pulled his phone from his pocket and called the hotel's owner, Enrique, before he made a thorough search among the bushes and trees surrounding the pool terrace. As he'd expected, whoever had been hiding there had gone. Minutes later, he heard a voice behind him.

'Paloma has returned to the penthouse. I have assigned a security guard to patrol the corridor outside the suite,' Enrique told him. 'What's the problem?'

'Someone knows she is here.'

'I don't see how that is possible. You were both checked into the hotel under false names. Do you think one of the other guests recognised Paloma?'

'The only time she left the suite was tonight when she came down to the pool.' Daniele's jaw clenched. He would have tried to stop her if he'd known she planned to swim. Fear had cramped in his stomach when he'd discovered that Paloma was not in her room.

'I've stepped up security around the hotel,' Enrique said. 'Do you still believe that one or more of the trustees of her grandfather's company want Paloma out of the way?'

'It's an undeniable fact that they would all benefit financially. Her great-uncle has made no secret that he wants control of Morante Group, but would he arrange to have Paloma kidnapped?'

'Money and power are strong motivators. What about you, Daniele? What is the motivation for your involvement with Paloma?'

'I promised her grandfather as he was dying that I would take care of her.'

Enrique chuckled. 'Keep telling yourself that, my friend. I have seen the way you look at this woman.'

'You are imagining things,' Daniele drawled. 'Marriage and babies have made you soft.'

'I admit I'm crazy in love with my wife. You should try it.'

Daniele snorted. 'I saw what being in love did to my father. He never got over my mother leaving.'

As Daniele walked back to the hotel, his mind was on his parents' marriage, which had been doomed from the start, according to his grandmother. Nonna Elsa had described his mother as having had airs and graces, and she'd thought herself too good to live in the cramped apartment that had been all Daniele's father could afford.

Claudia Farnesi's brief infatuation with a handsome soldier had resulted in pregnancy and a marriage that had been against her aristocratic family's wishes. She had abandoned her husband and young son and returned to a life of wealth and luxury. But Daniele knew his father had never stopped loving his mother, and he'd watched the once happy man become sad and bitter. Why would anyone risk their heart and happiness on such a fickle emotion as love? Daniele brooded. Love was a weakness and he had never understood its appeal.

They flew to Italy the next morning on a private jet that Daniele had chartered and landed at Pisa airport, where a chauffeured limousine was waiting to take them to Livorno. The sea-port was one of the largest in the Mediterra-nean. Years ago, Marcello had bought a fleet of six cargo ships and established Morante Shipping as a subsidiary company of Morante Group. Livorno was also home to the barracks of the Italian special forces regiment that Daniele had once belonged to. Coming back to the town always evoked memories of his time as a soldier, and he still missed the army that had become his family and given him a sense of belonging.

The car headed towards the historic old town and drew up in front of a grand, neoclassical building that housed Morante Group's head-quarters. Paloma had barely said a word since they had left Tunisia, but now Daniele heard her catch her breath.

'The press conference is arranged for mid-day,' he told her. 'Franco has offered to make the public announcement of Marcello's death if you feel unable to.'

'I'll do it. I am my grandfather's successor and I want to pay tribute to him. It feels strange coming here, knowing that Nonno is not in his office. I don't think it has really sunk in yet that I will never see him again.' Her voice was unsteady.

Daniele shifted closer to her, intending to

place his hand over hers, but he thought better of it and leaned back in his seat. Comforting Paloma had not gone to plan when he had found her by the pool, he reminded himself derisively.

Last night she had looked young and impossibly innocent, with her wet hair hanging down her back and her face bare of make-up. Today she was the epitome of elegance, in a black sheath dress that emphasised her slim figure. Vertiginous stiletto heels drew attention to her long legs, and her handbag bore the distinctive MGL logo of the Morante Group leather accessories range. Her hair was swept up in a chignon and her face was discreetly made up. A pair of oversized sunglasses shielded her expression, but Daniele sensed that her grief for her grandfather was raw when they entered the office building from where Marcello had amassed his business empire.

They went straight to the hospitality suite where members of the press had gathered. Paloma was composed when she gave a statement announcing the sudden death of Marcello Morante, the founder of Morante Group and the Morante Foundation, a renowned philanthropist and her beloved grandfather.

'Signorina Morante, can you confirm who is to replace Marcello?' a journalist asked.

'I will become the head of Morante Group when I am twenty-five. Until then, according to the terms of my grandfather's will, all decisions pertaining to the company will be made jointly by myself and the board of trustees.'

'Are you concerned about taking on the enormous responsibility of running the company when you are so young and inexperienced in business?'

'I am my grandfather's heir. It was his wish that I would succeed him, and I will do my best to honour his faith in me.' Paloma stood up and cast her cool gaze over the group of journalists before she swept out of the room. Her regal bearing denoted her aristocratic heritage as the granddaughter of a marchese. But Daniele knew she would need more than her impressive family background to win the support of the board. He opened the door of the boardroom and stood aside to allow Paloma to precede him into the room.

The eight trustees sitting around the table were all male, and all were getting on in years, Daniele surmised. Marcello's loyalty to his old friends, even though a few of them should have long since retired, had been his one weakness. Morante Group would benefit from the new ideas and fresh approach that Paloma might bring, but could she count on the support of the board? Raised voices had been audible from the corridor and it had sounded as though a fierce debate had been taking place. Paloma's arrival prompted an awkward silence.

Franco Zambrotta stood up and crossed the room. 'Paloma, my dear,' he greeted her warmly, but Daniele was not taken in by the other man's smile that did not reach his eyes. 'It was good of you to leave your home in England...' Franco's hesitation was deliberate, to remind the other trustees that Paloma did not live in Italy '...and come here to give a charming public tribute to Marcello. I speak for all the trustees when I say that we understand how devastated you must be at his death. You are not in the right state of mind to make decisions about your future with the company.'

Paloma tensed, and Daniele wanted to tell Franco to give her a break. He hadn't expected the other man would show his hand so early. 'There is nothing wrong with my state of mind, Tio Franco,' Paloma said crisply as she walked up to the chair at the head of the table where her grandfather had used to sit. 'My future with Morante Group is not up for debate. Nonno's will clearly states that he wanted me to succeed him.'

'I am certain that Marcello expected to live for many more years, and he would have trained you to eventually take his place.' Franco's smile had disappeared when he returned to his seat. 'The trustees have been discussing whether I, as the president of the board, should take charge of Morante Group.'

'But that would be going against my grandfather's wishes,' Paloma argued.

One of the other trustees, Gianluca Orsi, spoke. 'We had the greatest respect for Marcello. But his affection for you, his only grandchild, meant that he overlooked your lack of business experience and your impulsiveness. For instance, your decision to marry without ensuring that your assets were protected.'

Before Paloma could respond, Franco said gravely, 'There is another, more serious matter. It has been brought to my attention that you have a personal involvement with the vice president of the board.'

Daniele glanced at Paloma's puzzled expression. His eyes narrowed as he looked at the projector screen on the wall where an image had appeared. Now he had proof that there had been a person hiding in the bushes next to the hotel pool in Tunisia. His gut clenched at the thought that whoever had been there last night could have aimed a gun at Paloma instead of a camera lens. Had someone paid whoever had taken the damning photo of him and Paloma? And could that someone be Franco?

'The photograph was sent to me by an anonymous source.' Franco looked around the table at the other trustees. 'You can imagine the damage that would be caused to the reputation of Morante Group if the press got hold of the picture and published it.'

CHAPTER FOUR

PALOMA FELT AS though she was trapped in an endless nightmare. Her kidnap ordeal, her grandfather's unexpected death and now this. She squeezed her eyes shut and prayed that the image of her and Daniele wasn't real. But when she cautiously lifted her lashes, the picture on the screen was still in front of her. The photo had been blown up to almost life-size and appeared to show them sharing an intimate moment beside the swimming pool in Tunisia.

Daniele's arms were wrapped around her waist, while her body, clad in a skimpy swimsuit, was pressed up against him. But it was the yearning expression on her face that made Paloma wish she could sink into the thick pile carpet on the boardroom floor. The photo had captured her in an unguarded moment when her lips had been parted in an invitation for Daniele to kiss her.

She felt too embarrassed to look at him. She was conscious of the disapproving glances from the group of men around the table and her face grew warm. 'It's not what it looks like,' she stammered.

Franco crashed his hand down on the table, making Paloma flinch. 'What it looks like is a gross breach of policy with regard to the professional conduct of employees and representatives of the company. If the photograph were made public, I have no doubt the shareholders would be horrified by the evidence that you are having a casual affair with Daniele and the disrespect you have both shown for Marcello, days after his death and before he has been laid to rest. To protect the good name of Morante Group, I propose that the board should vote against you succeeding Marcello and appoint me as chairman with immediate effect.'

For a moment Paloma seriously considered if she should walk away from the company as her uncle and the rest of the board clearly hoped she would do. The trustees were elderly men who were set in their ways and likely to oppose any new ideas she tried to introduce. It would be easier to hand power over to Franco.

Maybe she wasn't good enough to take her grandfather's place anyway. Doubt piled upon doubt as her old insecurities surfaced. She'd never been good enough for her mother, who had wanted Paloma to be a party-loving socialite, and she hadn't been good enough for Calum,

who had married her when he'd been in love
with someone else.

But she had meant everything to Nonno.
Paloma had never doubted her grandfather's
love for her, and she owed it to him to fight
with every means at her disposal for her right
to succeed him as the head of the company and
the charitable foundation that he had worked
tirelessly for. The jumble of thoughts inside her
head cleared, and she sucked in a deep breath
as she prepared to take the biggest gamble of
her life.

'It's not a casual affair. I am going to marry
Daniele,' she blurted out. Nine pairs of eyes
swung in her direction, but she was only conscious of his glittering amber gaze focused in-
tently on her. 'We have had…feelings for each
other for quite a while.' Paloma knew that if her
plan backfired she was going to look very foolish in front of the board, whom she needed to
impress. 'Naturally, my fiancé was the person
I turned to for comfort while I grieved for my
grandfather.'

'Is this true?' Franco asked Daniele. 'Marcello never mentioned that you are engaged to
his granddaughter.'

Paloma held her breath, remembering her
angry response when Daniele had suggested she
should marry him. How she regretted her stupid pride. He had been right when he'd warned

her that her great-uncle was determined to seize control of the company. Her future at Morante Group was in Daniele's hands.

Her gaze dropped to his strong, tanned hands resting on the table. Hands that had burned through her swimsuit when he'd held her against his whipcord body. But his touch had been unexpectedly gentle when he had run his fingers through her hair. She forced her eyes up to his face and wished she knew what he was thinking behind his enigmatic expression. His silence stretched her nerves to snapping point.

'I trust you are not implying that my fiancée is lying, Franco,' Daniele said curtly. 'Marcello's sudden death was a shock to all of us. Paloma and I decided to postpone announcing our engagement because of the deep respect we both felt for her grandfather.' His voice was icy, and Paloma could have sworn that the temperature in the boardroom had dropped by several degrees.

Daniele fixed his hard stare on each of the trustees in turn. 'Your concerns about Paloma succeeding her grandfather are unfounded. I will support and guide her in preparation for when she takes control of Morante Group on her twenty-fifth birthday. You are all aware that when I established the company's online presence, new markets were opened up in Asia and profits soared. Marcello demonstrated his trust in me by appointing me as a lifelong member of the board. Now I am asking you to trust that, with Paloma as my wife, we will work as a team to take the company forwards to an exciting and successful future.'

God, he was good! Paloma was almost convinced of Daniele's sincerity, and it was evident from the approving nods from many of the trustees that he had won them over. Nonno had joked that Daniele could sell wine to a vintner, she remembered ruefully. She must not forget that his marriage proposition was a cold-blooded arrangement that would benefit both of them.

Daniele stood up and walked around the table towards Paloma. She could not tear her gaze from him. His elegant suit was undoubtedly bespoke, and the superb tailoring drew attention to his broad shoulders and long, lean frame. The sensual musk of his cologne evoked an ache low in her pelvis.

Her eyes widened when he drew her to her feet and lifted her hand up to his lips. He brushed his mouth lightly over her knuckles, and a sensation like an electrical current shot through her fingers and up her arm. She felt her nipples pinch and prayed they were not visible beneath her dress.

'I am sorry, *carissima*, that events have forced us to reveal our marriage plans,' Daniele murmured. His eyes gleamed when he met Paloma's startled gaze. 'You are the only woman on the planet who I want to marry.'

She blushed when he gave her a mocking smile, but she needed his help, and so she resisted the temptation to grind her stiletto heel into his foot. 'And you are the only man for me, *caro*,' she simpered. Daniele's lips twitched, but when he turned to address the board of trustees, his expression was serious.

'We had intended to wait until after Marcello's funeral before revealing our relationship. The photograph is an invasion of our privacy, and I will call in private investigators to try and discover who was behind the attempt to discredit us.' Daniele's eyes narrowed on Franco before he continued. 'Paloma chose not to wear an engagement ring until our relationship became public, but now there is no reason for me to wait to put my ring on her finger.'

With mounting disbelief, Paloma watched as Daniele reached into the inside pocket of his jacket and withdrew a small leather pouch. The ring he tipped into his palm was poignantly familiar. An oval-shaped sapphire surrounded by diamonds, it had belonged to her grandmother who had died before Paloma was born. Her grandfather had treasured the ring, and she had no idea how Daniele had come to have it in his possession.

'Paloma, *tesoro mio*,' Daniele murmured. She

froze when she realised that he was actually going to propose to her right there in the boardroom. His deep voice was as soft as a velvet cloak against her skin. 'Will you marry me and make me the happiest man in the world?'

She knew that Daniele was putting on an act, and there was no explanation for why her pulse was racing. Paloma's mind flew back to when her ex-husband had proposed. Calum had used every cliché. A romantic dinner at her favourite restaurant, a bouquet of red roses, and he had even dropped down onto one knee when he'd presented her with a ring, but not his heart, she had discovered soon after the wedding. Would she ever receive a marriage proposal from a man who loved her for herself? she wondered with a pang.

She forced herself to smile at Daniele. 'I will.'

For some reason, her hand trembled when he slid the ring onto her finger. Incredibly, it fitted perfectly. Paloma stared at the exquisite piece of jewellery and felt an urge to tear it off. Marcello had given the ring to her grandmother, and theirs had been a true love match. The pretence that she and Daniele were in love felt like a travesty of the deep emotional bond between her grandparents that had been evident in their wedding photographs. Nonno had loved his wife for his entire life, even though her death had parted them far too soon, and he had never remarried.

The gentle ripple of applause from at least some of the trustees jolted Paloma from her thoughts, and her heart missed a beat when she discovered that Daniele had moved closer to her. He placed his hands on her waist and drew her towards him. Her breath became trapped in her throat when she realised his intention. His amber eyes were focused on her mouth as he dipped his head and brushed his lips across hers.

The kiss was over almost as soon as it had begun, but it seared Paloma down to her soul. She fleetingly tasted Daniele's warm breath, and his raw, male scent evoked a sharp tug of desire in the pit of her stomach. When he lifted his head, it was all she could do not to cling to him. The unsatisfactory kiss had left her aching for him to claim her mouth with hungry passion as he had done three years ago.

'Bravo!' Gianluca heaved himself rather stiffly to his feet, and most of the other trustees followed suit and offered their congratulations. Only Franco and the two men on either side of him said nothing.

'I am curious, Daniele, to know how you will prepare Paloma for leadership of Morante Group at the same time as running your e-commerce company,' Franco said tersely. 'You cannot be in two places at once.'

'I have an excellent executive team working for me at Premio.' Daniele shrugged. 'My business interests are varied, but for the past ten years, I have been involved in some way with Morante Group and the Morante Foundation.'

He looked at Paloma. 'The first decision you and the board must make is whether to cancel the charity foundation's gala ball that is meant to take place next weekend, two days after Marcello's funeral. Will it be too soon to host what is essentially a celebration while you are still mourning your grandfather?'

'Nonno would have wanted the ball to go ahead,' Paloma said with conviction. 'All the tickets have been sold, and refunds will have to be given if we cancel. The event raises a huge amount of money for the Morante Foundation and the many charitable causes it supports.'

Daniele nodded and turned to the trustees. 'I suggest a show of hands if you agree with Paloma.'

The vote was carried unanimously, although Franco had been the last to raise his hand, Paloma remembered after the board meeting had finished and she and Daniele were in the car on the way to her grandfather's palazzo, a few miles along the coast in the pretty resort of Tirrenia.

She simply could not believe that her great-uncle or any of the other trustees had been behind her kidnapping in Mali. Everything that had happened in the past few days seemed unreal. It felt like a lifetime ago that she had been teaching at a school in one of the poorest regions of Africa. Now she was the heiress to an enormous fortune and, thanks to Daniele, her position in Morante Group was more secure. But she'd had to agree to a fake engagement to the sexiest and most infuriatingly enigmatic man she had ever met.

She glanced at him, sitting beside her in the back of the limousine. Like her, Daniele had not spoken since they'd left Morante Group's offices, and he seemed to be lost in his thoughts. Paloma studied his chiselled profile, and her heart skipped a beat when he turned his head and caught her staring at him.

'That will be something to tell our grandchildren,' he drawled.

'What will?' She gave him a puzzled look.

'The story of how in the middle of a board meeting you propositioned me to marry you.' He grinned at her affronted expression. 'And how, to save you from embarrassment, I officially proposed.'

'Marriage was your idea. You know I only agreed to it to stop Franco seizing control of the company,' she said sharply. 'I don't *want* to be engaged to you. Obviously, we are not going to have any children and therefore grandchildren.'

'Don't you want to have a family of your own?'

An image flashed into Paloma's mind, of

herself cradling a baby with jet-black hair and amber eyes. Daniele's son. She shook her head, feeling hot-faced and flustered, aware that he had been teasing her. 'Perhaps I will have children one day. But it's beside the point. We don't have to get married.'

Daniele raised an eyebrow. 'We don't?'

'All we have to do is keep up the pretence that we're engaged until I am twenty-five, when I can take charge of Morante Group as Nonno's will states. My birthday is in eight months. It's not unusual for couples to take a year or more to plan the perfect wedding, and it won't seem odd if we announce that we will marry next year.'

'By which time, you will have inherited your grandfather's company, and no one on the board of trustees will be able to make a leadership challenge.'

'Exactly.' Paloma gave a sigh of relief that Daniele saw the sense in what she was saying.

'You seem to have forgotten that we made a marriage bargain,' he reminded her. 'I stated my terms for helping you and I expect you to marry me. You will be able to claim your place as the head of Morante Group, and I will have an aristocratic wife with a pedigree that goes back centuries.'

'You make me sound like a thoroughbred broodmare,' she muttered.

Daniele gave her an amused look. 'You are much prettier than a horse, *cara*.'

Those mesmerising amber eyes of his glowed like the embers of a fire. Heat surged through Paloma at the startling idea that he was flirting with her. His throwaway *'cara'* tugged on her heart, even though she told herself he probably used the affectionate term with his—if the gossip columns were to be believed—legions of lovers.

'Why do you want a wife with a title?' she asked him. 'You told me that it mattered to your mother, but why do you care what she thinks after she abandoned you when you were a child?'

Daniele looked uncomfortable and raked his hand through his hair. 'I suppose it was seeing reports in the newspapers that my grandfather had died, and my half-brother has succeeded him as the new Conte.' He shrugged. 'Pride drives me to want to remind my mother that she has another son besides Stefano and to show her that I have made a success of my life without her support. There is another reason why it is vital that we marry.' Daniele's voice hardened. 'The prenuptial agreement stating that I will not receive any of your money or possessions when we divorce must be kept a secret. Publicly we will let it be known that if something should happen to you, I will inherit the fortune left to you by your grandfather and automatically become the head of Morante Group.'

Daniele lifted his hand and captured her chin between his fingers, gently turning her head so that her eyes met his. 'I need you to trust me, Paloma. As your husband, I will be your next of kin, and anyone thinking of threatening your life in order to get hold of your inheritance will have to get rid of me too. But I won't let anything happen to you,' he said quickly when she gasped.

'Do you really believe I am in danger?' Paloma felt sick when Daniele nodded. The idea that someone valued her inheritance and control of the company more than her life was a crushing blow to her already shaky self-esteem. She wished she could hide away on a remote island, but if she turned her back on Morante Group, whoever had arranged for her to be kidnapped would have won. 'Marriage to me could put your life in danger. Why would you be prepared to risk your safety?' she asked Daniele huskily.

'My final words to your grandfather before he died were to promise to protect you. Like you, I have no wish to marry, but I'm afraid there is no other way.'

Daniele could not have made it any clearer that he would prefer to walk barefoot through a pit of vipers than walk up the aisle with her. His incentive was that she was the Morante heiress, and he hoped that by marrying her, he would gain his mother's acceptance. Paloma stared at the ring he had placed on her finger. An engagement ring was meant to be a symbol of love and commitment, but for all its beauty, the sapphire ring was a reminder of the marriage bargain she had made with a man who regarded her as his duty and nothing more.

'Was it by chance that you came to the board meeting prepared, or had you planned to announce our engagement to the trustees?' She held out her left hand and, in the bright sunshine streaming through the car window, the diamonds surrounding the sapphire sparkled with fiery brilliance. 'I am curious as to why you gave me this particular ring.'

'I'm sure you know that Marcello always carried your grandmother's engagement ring with him, as he did on the day we played golf together. He gave me the ring when we were in the ambulance and said he wanted you to have it.' Daniele frowned. 'Your grandfather could not have foreseen the circumstances in which I presented you with the ring, but I believe he would understand that a fake engagement and marriage are the best way I can protect you.'

Daniele knew he had not been completely truthful with Paloma about the ring. He stared unseeingly out of the car window, remembering when

Marcello had pressed a small leather pouch into his hand.

'I will soon be with my beloved Isabella,' the dying man had rasped. 'I have kept her ring next to my heart since she was taken from me. You have it now, and one day you will give the ring to the woman who possesses your heart.'

It was never going to happen, Daniele brooded. He would not allow his heart to be possessed by any woman. Although the circumstances had been different, both his father and Marcello had lost the women they'd loved, and they had been heartbroken for the rest of their lives. Daniele did not want to be consumed by a grand passion. He preferred to be in control of his life and his emotions.

It was right that Paloma should have her grandmother's engagement ring. He had kept it in his jacket pocket, intending to give it to her before her grandfather's funeral. But when Franco had seemed poised to take control of Morante Group, Daniele had needed to act fast, to convince the board of trustees that he would marry Paloma and prepare her for when she succeeded Marcello as the head of the company.

The car slowed as it approached the entrance to the grounds of the palazzo. Daniele was puzzled when he saw that the ornate iron gates were open and there was no security guard in the gatehouse. A sweeping driveway lined with slender cypress trees led to the palatial building that had been the home of the noble Morante family since the sixteenth century.

Paloma climbed out of the car and preceded Daniele up the flight of stone steps to the front door. 'It feels as though the place has been abandoned,' she said with a catch in her voice. 'I suppose it's my imagination because I know that Nonno won't stride out of his study to greet me.'

The door was opened by the butler. 'There is only me and my wife, Giulia, here to take care of the house,' Aldo explained when Paloma and Daniele stepped into the opulent entrance hall. 'Yesterday, all the other household staff received letters informing them that they no longer had their jobs. I have just seen a news report on the television that Signor Morante is dead. Please accept my condolences, *signorina.*'

'It must be a mistake,' Paloma said. 'My grandfather would not have wanted his staff who had worked for him for years to be sacked. Who sent the dismissal letters?'

'They had been signed by Signor Morante. Everyone was upset because your grandfather had not given any indication that he was displeased with the staff.'

'But Nonno died a week ago.' Paloma looked at Daniele. 'He couldn't have sacked the staff. So who did?'

'What about the security team?' Daniele asked the butler. 'Were they dismissed too?'

Aldo nodded. 'With the announcement of Signor Morante's death, I am concerned that thieves might try to break into the house while there are no security personnel patrolling the grounds.'

'It's a bit odd, isn't it?' Paloma muttered as she followed Daniele into the salon.

The dismissal of the security staff was more than odd. The hairs on the back of Daniele's neck prickled. 'It's not safe for you to stay at the palazzo. I'm guessing you keep clothes here for when you visit.' She nodded, and he said briskly, 'Go and change your clothes and pack a bag.' He pulled out his phone. 'I need to make alternative arrangements.'

'This is my home now and I won't be scared away from it,' Paloma said in a determined voice. 'Besides, the charity ball will be held here, and I need to help with the preparations. My grandfather always took a personal interest in the fundraising event.' She bit her lip. 'If you really think that someone on the board of trustees wants me...out of the way, we ought to call the police.'

'And tell them what? For all we know, your grandfather might have decided to sack the staff and signed the dismissal letters before he died. They would have taken a few days to arrive in the post.' Daniele could not hide his frustration. 'No actual threat has been made against you while you have been in Italy and the police will not have the authority to investigate your kidnapping in Mali. You are my responsibility.'

Daniele could tell from the way Paloma's eyes had darkened to indigo that an argument was brewing. 'I will rehire the palazzo's staff and the security team in time for the charity ball, but until then, I'm taking you to my farmhouse near Lucca. Be ready to leave in half an hour.'

'Are you always so overbearing?' Paloma gave him a mutinous look. 'I appreciate your help, but I don't want you to think of me as your responsibility.'

It was vital that he did, Daniele brooded. Otherwise his thoughts might turn to how desperately he wanted to kiss Paloma's lips, which were currently set in a sulky pout. When he'd grazed his mouth over hers at the board meeting, it had taken all his willpower to resist deepening the kiss. But even the brief taste of her sweet breath had had an instant effect on his body, and he'd quickly stepped away from her before she had become aware of his rampant arousal.

Things were likely to get worse once they were married, he acknowledged grimly. In public they would have to put on a convincing act that their marriage was real to keep Morante Group's shareholders happy. Daniele's gaze was drawn to Paloma's pert derrière when she turned and walked away from him. He cursed beneath his breath. *Deal with one problem at a time*, he told himself. Right now he needed to take her to where he could keep her safe while he tried to discover what the hell was going on.

'What is happening?' Paloma asked some forty minutes later when she emerged from the car and stared at the crash helmet Daniele held out to her. He had driven them from the palazzo to a garage in a nearby village.

'We'll swap vehicles and travel to the farmhouse on the bike in case anyone is looking out for the car. Here's a leather jacket for you to wear. It should fit.'

'I suppose another of your ex-army friends left the motorbike and gear here for us,' she said drily. 'It's a good thing I'm wearing my jeans.'

The sight of Paloma's sexy figure in skintight denim was not a good thing for Daniele's blood pressure. Earlier in the day, she had looked sophisticated and untouchable in a designer outfit. Now her long hair was loose and spilled down her back like a curtain of silk. The leather jacket she'd slipped on gave her an edgy, rock-chick look that made Daniele's hands itch to touch every gorgeous inch of her.

'Climb onto the back of the bike and put your arms around my waist,' he growled, before he jammed his helmet onto his head and started the motorbike's powerful engine.

The sun was setting, and the Tuscan scenery was breathtaking, with the undulating hills dappled in gold and the pointed spires of the cypress trees casting long shadows. Daniele felt his tension ease and he relished the sense of freedom he felt on the motorbike as he opened up the throttle. He should spend more time out of the office, he brooded.

For the past decade, he had been driven by his determination to make his fortune, and deep down, he'd hoped that his mother would admire his achievements. He had told Paloma it was pride that made him want to impress his mother, but he acknowledged that he was still haunted by her rejection. If his mother hadn't loved him, would any woman truly love him? He'd told himself he did not want love in his life, but there was an emptiness inside him that money and success could not fill.

His self-made wealth had not gained him Claudia Farnesi's acceptance. But marriage to Paloma would make him a member of one of the most prestigious families in Italy and give him status in the highest echelons of society. Surely, his mother would be impressed by the son she had abandoned when Daniele had been a boy?

CHAPTER FIVE

'WELCOME TO MY HOME,' Daniele said after he'd parked the bike in front of the farmhouse and dismounted.

'This is beautiful.' Paloma removed her crash helmet and swung her leg over the saddle. 'No one would guess the house was here, nestled between the hills. There's not another building for miles.' She turned her stunning blue eyes towards him. 'I had you down as a city type, and I've seen photos of you emerging from nightclubs and casinos in the early hours with your latest mistress wrapped around you,' she said with some asperity.

Daniele grinned. 'There is no need to be jealous, *cara*. When we are married, I will be exclusively yours.'

'I'm not *jealous*.' Two patches of scarlet flared on Paloma's cheeks. 'I couldn't care less what you get up to in your private life.'

'Neither of us will have a private life for the next few months.' His tone became serious.

'Our marriage must appear to be real, which means that I am the only man you can be associated with.'

'*I* don't have hordes of admirers.' She grimaced. 'Not genuine ones, anyway.'

'What do you mean?'

'When men look at me, they see a cash cow.'

'That's not true.' Daniele had heard genuine hurt behind her flippant remark, and a hot tide of anger swept through him. Who had made Paloma feel that she was only valued for the size of her inheritance? Had it been her ex-husband? Daniele did not know the reason why her marriage had broken up, but there had been wild speculation in the British press over the size of the financial settlement Paloma had given her ex.

She had become a millionairess at eighteen when she'd taken control of the trust fund left to her by her father, who had died two years earlier. Now she had inherited her grandfather's vast fortune. Daniele frowned when he remembered that Paloma believed everyone wanted something from her. Was he any better? his conscience demanded. He was not interested in her money, but he wanted the position in society that being married to Paloma would give him.

'Why did you choose to live in the middle of nowhere?'

'Actually, I don't spend as much time here

as I would like. My business is based in Rome and I have an apartment in the city. But I was drawn to the remoteness and tranquillity of this place. Like many soldiers who were sent to war zones, I value peace.'

'I didn't realise you had served abroad. Where did you go?'

'Afghanistan.' Memories flashed through Daniele's mind. The heat and dust, the constant threat from IEDs, his own very personal dread of being shot dead by a sniper. Like father, like son. He took a deep breath and pushed away thoughts of his best friend, Gino, who had not returned home from war.

The farmhouse was his sanctuary, and Paloma was the only woman he had ever brought here. But he'd reasoned that it would be easier to keep her hidden in the heart of rural Tuscany than if he took her to Rome or Florence. He ushered her into the house and wondered what she would make of its rustic charm after the opulence of the Morante palazzo. Why did he care what Paloma thought? Daniele wondered irritably. He did not need to impress her. Their marriage bargain would benefit her as much as it would him.

'I don't employ any full-time staff here,' he explained. 'A woman from the village comes in a couple of times a week to keep the place clean. The freezer is always well stocked, and

I've arranged for someone to deliver fresh produce. You are probably used to being waited on by servants, but you'll have to muck in. I can cook, although nothing more adventurous than steak and eggs.'

Paloma followed him into the bright kitchen, where an old-fashioned range stood against one wall. The wooden table in the centre of the room looked as ancient as the house. 'You can leave the catering to me. My grandfather insisted that I spent six months at a Swiss finishing school, and I learned cordon bleu cookery as well as the many other accomplishments expected of an aristocratic bride. That's the reason you are going to marry me, after all,' she said drily.

Daniele met her limpid gaze and laughed despite himself. The attraction that had simmered between them since he'd rescued her in Africa sparked into a blaze. Three years ago, Paloma had been shy, and her obvious crush on him had been distracting. He had been determined to ignore the chemistry between them, telling himself that she was too young and inexperienced. He'd felt sure that her grandfather would not approve if he'd had a relationship with Paloma, and so he had avoided her as much as possible. Until he'd kissed her back at the ball and been forced to admit to himself that he'd avoided her for an entirely different reason—that she tested his self-control to its limits.

Since then, Paloma had developed a strong will and a fieriness that Daniele admired. Added to that, she was the sexiest woman he had ever laid eyes on. An erotic image flashed into his mind of Paloma naked and spread across the kitchen table, her long hair tumbling over her breasts and her lips set in a pout that he would enjoy teasing apart with his tongue.

Dio! He turned away from her and pretended to study the bottles in the wine rack to hide the betraying bulge in the front of his jeans. His role was to protect her, he reminded himself. He had discovered a vulnerability to Paloma that warned him to keep his distance.

'You have a lot of misconceptions about me,' she murmured. 'While I was at university, I lived in student digs, and in Mali, my accommodation was basic. I shared a bedroom with a family of cockroaches.'

Daniele knew he should go to his study and switch on his computer. He had several major deals in the pipeline, and usually he would be impatient to get back to work. Instead he opened a bottle of Chianti, found a couple of glasses and pulled out a chair at the table while he watched Paloma investigate the kitchen cupboards and fridge and assemble a pile of ingredients for dinner.

'Why did you go to Africa? Was it simply a

laudable desire to help underprivileged children, or were you running away?'

She flushed. 'Perceptive, aren't you? Volunteering as a teacher in Mali was important to me. But you're right—it gave me a chance to escape from the fallout of my divorce. I felt so stupid that I had been taken in by Calum's lies.' Paloma picked up a knife and chopped some mushrooms with unnecessary force.

'Why did you marry him?'

'I thought I loved him and that he loved me. I was wrong on both counts.' She drank some wine. 'The short version of the story is that Calum was in love with another woman. I discovered later that their relationship had broken up shortly before I met him. He was a barman at a pub near to the London offices of the charity where I worked.'

Paloma paused and took another sip of her drink. 'Calum was handsome and fun to be with. He was unaware that I was an heiress, or so I thought.' She sighed. 'My mother never lets me forget that she is Lady Coulton, and that I am the granddaughter of an English earl and an Italian marchese. She was desperate for me to marry a man with a title. Nonno was putting pressure on me to move to Italy and work with him at Morante Group. When I eloped with Calum, it seemed romantic and exciting, but soon after I'd married him, I realised I had made a mistake when I discovered that he had deliberately fooled me.'

She drained her glass and pushed it across the table for Daniele to refill it. 'Calum *had* known that I was wealthy after an Italian barman at the pub recognised I was the Morante heiress. He was attracted to my money, but a few days before our wedding, his ex-girlfriend told him that she was pregnant with his baby. Obviously, I knew nothing about it then. Calum went ahead and married me, anticipating that he could expect a sizeable divorce settlement.'

Paloma took another long sip of wine. 'I'd stupidly married him without a prenuptial agreement because I believed we would be together for ever. But weeks after the wedding, he resumed his relationship with his girlfriend. Their baby was born a few months later while Calum was still technically my husband.'

Daniele frowned. 'Under those circumstances, it was reasonable for you to file for divorce. Your husband had never been committed to the marriage and I am surprised that a judge awarded him a financial settlement.'

'I didn't fight his claim for money in court.' A pink stain spread over Paloma's face. 'Calum had some raunchy photographs of me on his phone. When we were dating, he'd persuaded me to take pictures of myself in the nude and send them to him. I know, I was an idiot,' she muttered when Daniele swore softly. 'He'd promised he would never show them to anyone. Calum agreed to a quick divorce if I gave him the house in London that I'd bought as our marital home, plus an additional financial settlement. If I refused, he said he would pass the photos to the tabloids.'

Daniele discovered that he had unconsciously clenched his fists as he imagined meeting Paloma's ex-husband. 'You could have had him charged with blackmail, which carries a prison sentence.'

'I couldn't risk the pictures being made public. My grandfather would have been horrified, and I couldn't face further humiliation. I just wanted out of the marriage, so I agreed to Calum's terms.' She gave a bitter laugh. 'Now you know the miserable details of my marriage and why I am in no rush to do it again.'

Once again, Daniele's conscience pricked that he would benefit from marrying Paloma. The situation was not the same as her first marriage, he assured himself. He'd been honest with her and he had not pretended that their marriage would be anything other than a business arrangement. But now more than ever he was determined to ignore his inconvenient attraction to her. He could not risk any kind of involvement with Paloma that she might misconstrue as something more than sexual desire.

He left her to prepare dinner while he went to unstrap their bags from the back of the motorbike and carry them upstairs to the bedrooms. When he returned to the kitchen, Paloma was serving up mushroom risotto. She had tied her long hair in a ponytail, and her cheeks were flushed from the heat of the range, and perhaps from the wine. Her glass was empty. Daniele opened a second bottle of Chianti. They could both do with loosening up after the fraught past few days.

While they ate, he kept the conversation on neutral topics. The dark smudges beneath Paloma's eyes were a sign of the strain she had been under recently. She had grown up used to a life of privilege, but there were no airs and graces to her, and she insisted on helping clear up the kitchen. Afterwards, she opted to watch a film in the sitting room. Daniele went to his study to call Enrique, who operated a security and private investigation business from his hotel in Tunisia.

Enrique had no further news on who had been behind Paloma's kidnapping, but he'd compiled detailed reports on the members of the board of trustees, their families and associates. Daniele skimmed through the information Enrique had emailed to him and frowned when he saw a name he thought he recognised.

'What do we know about Alberto Facchetti?'

'He is the son-in-law of one of the trustees, Gianluca Orsi. Facchetti owns a haulage business transporting freight through Europe. Do you want me to dig deeper?'

'*Sì, grazie.*'

Returning to the sitting room, Daniele halted in the doorway when he saw Paloma lying on the sofa. Her hair spilled over the cushions and her impossibly long eyelashes made dark fans on her porcelain skin. Her lips were slightly parted, and the steady rise and fall of her breasts beneath her clingy top indicated that she was deeply asleep.

Her intriguing mix of innocence and sensuality sent his pulse haywire. He considered covering her with a blanket and leaving her to spend the night on the sofa. But her neck was at an odd angle and she would be stiff in the morning. Swearing beneath his breath, Daniele lifted her into his arms.

She weighed next to nothing. Her hair felt like silk against his skin, and her perfume—something lightly floral mingled with muskier notes of amber wood and patchouli—evoked a dull throb in his groin. Jaw clenched, he carried her through the house and up the stairs to the second floor. Opposite the master suite was a guest bedroom with en suite bathroom. He shouldered the door and touched the switch on the wall to turn on the bedside lamp before he laid Paloma on the bed.

She had not stirred. Daniele looked at her skintight jeans and frowned. 'Paloma.' He gently shook her shoulder. 'You need to get undressed.'

Her lashes swept upwards, and she regarded him with her startlingly blue eyes. Deep enough for a man to drown in. 'Is that an invitation?'

'Of course it isn't,' he said curtly. He was furious with himself for his inability to control his body's response to Paloma's sleepy, sexy smile.

'Keep your hat on. I was joking.' She sat up and ran her fingers through her mass of chestnut hair. 'I know you are not attracted to me.'

'You know that, do you?' Daniele growled, fighting the temptation to show her how wrong she was.

Paloma rubbed her brow. 'Ow, my head. I think I may have drunk too much wine.' She tilted her head to one side and fixed her mesmerising gaze on him. 'If you did find me attractive, you would have kissed me properly today, instead of acting like I have a highly contagious disease.' She giggled when he scowled. 'You'll have to do better to convince everyone that our marriage is real. Maybe you should practise kissing me.'

She would tempt a saint, let alone a mortal man. He tore his gaze from her lush mouth and stepped away from the bed. 'Tomorrow you will be glad that I would never take advantage of a woman who has had too much to drink,' Daniele drawled. 'I'll bring you some water. If you're going to be sick, make sure you get to the bathroom in time.'

Down in the kitchen, he opened the back door and dragged the cool night air into his lungs. He had made a promise to Marcello that he would protect Paloma, he reminded himself. This was just another mission. His special forces training had taught him to detach his emotions from a situation and focus on the job. He should not feel a violent urge to rearrange Paloma's ex-husband's features with his fist in retribution for how badly the guy had hurt her.

You must want something from me. Everyone always does.

How the hell was he supposed to remain detached after he had seen the wounded expression in Paloma's eyes? How had his life suddenly become so crazily complicated? Daniele wondered as he filled a jug with water.

When he went back upstairs and knocked on the door before entering her room, he caught a flash of white silk negligee and an expanse of slender, tanned thigh as she leapt into bed and pulled the covers up to her chin.

She watched him warily when he placed the jug on the bedside table. 'Thank you.'

'Goodnight.' He switched off the lamp and turned to walk out of the room.

'Daniele, don't go.'

He exhaled heavily. 'You are going to hate yourself in the morning, *cara*.'

'I'm scared the kidnappers will break into the house and seize me like they did in Mali.' Her voice shook, and her vulnerability felt like a knife in his heart.

'No one knows where you are,' he said gruffly.

'You said the same thing in Tunisia.'

The damn photograph. Who had been lurking in the bushes by the pool? A member of the paparazzi who'd got lucky when he'd spotted the Morante heiress? Or was there a more sinister reason why the photographer had been there? With a faint sigh, Daniele lowered himself into the armchair next to Paloma's bed. 'I won't let any harm come to you. Go to sleep, *piccola*.'

Oh, no! Paloma slowly opened her eyes and decided that death would be preferable to her pounding headache and the cringingly embarrassing memories of her behaviour the previous night. It was bad enough that she had bored Daniele with the humiliating details of her marriage. Thankfully, she hadn't told him everything. Her self-confidence had not recovered from Calum's rejection on their wedding night and her secret that she'd never confided to even her closest friend.

But she had confessed to Daniele about those awful photographs. Calum had been manipulative when he'd persuaded her to send him photos of herself in the shower. 'Sexting is part of a modern relationship,' he'd told her. 'Seeing pictures of your sexy body makes me feel closer to you.' Stupidly, she had believed his lies.

Paloma shoved the painful memories of her marriage back into the compartment in her mind marked *Do Not Open*. Goodness knew how many glasses of wine she'd drunk last night. The alcohol had made her feel relaxed and it must have gone straight to her head, but it did not excuse her suggestion that Daniele should practise kissing her.

He had looked appalled, and he'd shot out of her room faster than a cheetah that had spotted its lunch. But he had returned to reassure her that he would protect her. She turned her head on the pillow and felt relieved that he was not still sitting next to the bed.

She was ashamed of herself for being so pathetic. Her life had been spinning out of control for the past few days, but she had to get a grip, Paloma told herself sternly. It was not surprising that Daniele had accused her of being immature. How *could* she have asked him to stay with her? But her fear had been genuine. So many disturbing things had happened recently, and the dismissal of the security staff from the palazzo had been the final straw.

She staggered into the bathroom, and after she'd had a shower and swallowed a couple of painkillers, she felt almost human again. It was early in the morning, and the view out of the window of the soft mist over the hills, and the sky streaked with hues of pink and gold as the sun rose, urged her to go outside. She pulled on yoga pants and a matching bra top and braided her wet hair.

Stepping quietly out of her room, she looked across the hallway and saw that Daniele's bedroom door was open. He was sprawled on the bed, the sheet draped across his hips. The regular rise and fall of his chest told her that he was asleep. Her heart missed a beat as she wondered if he slept naked.

Get over him, she ordered herself. She would marry him because it was the only way she could prevent her great-uncle Franco from seizing control of her grandfather's company. But her fake marriage to Daniele would end on the day she turned twenty-five. She grimaced as she imagined the tabloid headlines when she divorced for a second time.

Unlucky in love! Or perhaps, *Money can't buy happiness!*

Both statements were true, she thought

bleakly. Although of course there was zero chance of her falling in love with Daniele.

In the kitchen, she made a fruit salad and added a dollop of thick yoghurt. Two cups of black coffee gave her the caffeine hit she craved, before she opened the door and stepped out into the courtyard, blinking in the bright sunshine.

A shadow fell across the cobblestones, and she froze in terror. Her heart felt as if it were about to explode inside her chest. Was the person hiding around the corner of the house planning to snatch her, or worse? Had they been sent by whoever had organised her kidnapping in Mali? Blinding white fury took over from her fear. She was tired of being a victim.

She remembered the advice from her martial arts, self-defence instructor. *Hit first, hit hard and run fast.*

It felt like a lifetime but her thought process had taken seconds. When the figure stepped out of the shadows, Paloma leapt forwards and brought her leg up, ramming her shin— the hardest part of her leg—into his groin. She heard him groan as he doubled over. The sun was in her eyes and she could not see his face. She held her left arm out in front of her in the block defence position and brought her other arm up to strike the assailant's throat with her clenched fist.

He grabbed her wrist, catching her off guard

so that she toppled to the ground with him, and her body landed on top of his. She yelped in pain when he forced her arm behind her back and captured her other hand in his as she tried to jab her fingers in his eye.

'You crazy wildcat!' Daniele's eyes blazed with fury. 'Where the hell did you learn Krav Maga techniques?'

'I didn't know it was you.' The adrenaline surging through Paloma fuelled her temper. 'Why were you creeping around? You were in bed asleep. I thought I was going to be attacked, so I attacked first.'

'You're lucky I didn't seriously hurt you. I may never father children,' Daniele muttered, wincing when her pelvic bone pressed against his groin. 'Your kick was right on target.'

She bit her lip. 'I'm sorry.'

'I go for a run most mornings. I didn't want to disturb you, so I left the house by the exterior stairs.'

Paloma glanced over at the set of stone steps on the side of the house and realised that they led directly up to his bedroom. She looked down at Daniele. Her shock was fading, and she was intensely aware of his muscular body beneath her. She noticed that the dark stubble on his jaw was thicker with a night's growth. His amber eyes gleamed with an intensity that made her wonder if he could read the thoughts inside her head. She hoped not, because those thoughts were inappropriate, considering their current position. Her tense muscles were softening, and it would be too easy to melt into him so that every dip and curve on her body fitted snugly to his lean frame.

'You can let me up,' she muttered.

'Not so fast.' He released her wrist that he'd been holding behind her back and moved his hand down to the base of her spine, clamping her against him. 'Tell me how a fragile English rose is proficient in a martial arts combat system developed by the Israeli army and used by military special forces in many countries.'

Her eyes flashed. 'I'm not fragile. I brought you down.'

'Only because I hadn't expected to be confronted by a ninja warrior.'

'*You* introduced me to Krav Maga years ago. I had been visiting my grandfather at the palazzo and he told me about the IT genius he'd employed to develop Morante Group's online marketing. Imagine my surprise when, instead of the computer nerd I was expecting, I saw a fit guy on the lawn, practising martial arts. You made it clear that you had no time for an annoying teenager, but you explained that Krav Maga combines boxing, judo and ju-jitsu.'

'You thought I was fit?'

She blushed. 'You know I did. When I left

boarding school and went to university, Nonno was concerned for my safety, and to keep him happy, I signed up for some self-defence classes. The local gym ran a Krav Maga course for women. Today was the first time I'd ever been in a situation where I was able to defend myself and I'm proud that I kept my nerve.'

Paloma felt empowered. She had been terrified when she'd thought an intruder was in the courtyard, but she'd pushed past her fear and used the self-defence techniques she had been taught. 'Obviously, if I'd known it was you, I wouldn't have gone into attack mode,' she told Daniele apologetically.

He moved suddenly and rolled them both over so that she was briefly lying beneath him before he stood up and offered her his hand to pull her to her feet. His eyes narrowed on her face, and she sensed that he was about to say something, but then he gave a slight shake of his head. 'You did well,' he said gruffly. Paloma felt ridiculously pleased by his praise. 'Come into the barn and show me what else you have learned.'

The barn must originally have been used to store farm equipment, but now it was a well-equipped gym. Daniele walked over to an area of the floor covered with thick mats. 'The best way for any woman—or man, for that matter—to keep safe is to avoid confrontation if possible.

That's especially true for someone of your petite build. There is no shame in running away.'

'I confronted you when I believed you were a threat, and I won,' she said indignantly.

'I hate to burst your bubble, but I knew it was you and I controlled my reaction. If I hadn't, I might have killed you,' he said grimly. 'As soon as you had delivered the kick, you should have run as fast as you could. However, it is true that the element of surprise can give vital minutes in which to escape from an attacker.' Daniele moved behind Paloma. 'Imagine that I am an assailant and I'm about to drag you into a dark alleyway. What are you going to do to get away from me?'

His arms shot around her in a bear hug, but she instantly dropped into a squat position, making it harder for him to pick her up. Remembering her training, she lunged forwards and at the same time thrust her elbow backwards into his abdomen.

'Good,' he grunted. 'The assailant would be off guard. But if he grabbed you like this—' Daniele seized her by her shoulder and spun her round to face him '—you'd have no choice but to defend yourself. Make a fist,' he instructed. 'Strike mainly with your top two knuckles. Go on, hit me in the stomach.'

Paloma stared at Daniele. She had been fascinated with him since she was a teenager.

However, none of her romantic daydreams had featured her punching him. 'I don't want to hurt you.'

He gave her a sardonic look. 'There's no chance of that happening.'

She sensed there had been a double meaning in his words to let her know she couldn't hurt him, either physically or on an emotional level. It infuriated her to admit that he could probably break her heart if she were ever foolish enough to allow him anywhere near that vital organ. She wanted to slap the arrogant expression off his face. Instead she drove her fist into his abdomen. It was like hitting a brick wall and he did not flinch.

'Again,' he said. 'An assailant would not be expecting you to show aggression. Fight like you mean it. Fight for your life, Paloma.'

For the next half an hour, Daniele alternately praised and criticised her as he put her through the hardest training session she'd ever done. She was breathing hard when he finally signalled that they had finished, but she noted that he was not in the least out of breath. He was a superb athlete. She leaned back against the wall and her gaze was drawn to Daniele's powerfully muscular body in grey running shorts and vest top. His skin was darkly tanned, and his legs and forearms were covered with fine black hairs that Paloma guessed also grew thickly over his chest.

He was blatantly masculine and utterly gorgeous. Her insides melted every time she looked at him. Their eyes met and held, and she sensed an undercurrent of awareness between them. There had been something raw and sexy about working out together and getting hot and sweaty. She understood why he had challenged her. He'd wanted her to react and let her anger out. Her marriage and divorce from Calum had robbed her of her self-worth. Being kidnapped, and the continuing threat to her safety, had made her feel disempowered. But Daniele had given her the opportunity to prove to herself that she was strong, mentally and physically.

He moved closer to her and laid his hand flat against the wall next to her head. His amber eyes glowed like the smouldering embers of a fire. 'I agree with the suggestion you made last night,' he murmured. 'Our marriage must appear to be genuine, and in public we will have to act as though we can't keep our hands off each other.'

His deep voice with its sexy accent sent a delicious shiver through Paloma. She licked her dry lips with the tip of her tongue. 'Do you mean you want to practise…kissing me? You didn't give that impression last night.'

'You'd had too much to drink, and I couldn't take advantage of you. But now…' His warm breath tickled her ear as he pulled her towards him and lowered his head. 'Will you object if I kiss you?'

She couldn't speak. Could barely breathe. He dominated all of her senses, and anticipation made her heart pound. His face was so close that she could count his eyelashes, but his mouth hovered tantalisingly out of reach. Realising that he was waiting for her to make a response, she gave a tiny shake of her head, and finally his lips met hers.

The kiss exploded through Paloma. Heat and fire. Her head fell back as she offered her lips to him, and he took everything and demanded more. This was nothing like the cool brush of his mouth over hers after he had announced their engagement at the board meeting. Daniele's arm tightened around her waist and he sank his other hand into her hair, drawing her against him so that she was conscious of his hard thighs and the tantalising ridges of his abdominal muscles.

He deepened the kiss, sliding his tongue over the shape of her lips before he dipped into her mouth in a flagrantly erotic exploration that drew a low moan from her throat. Paloma had *never* been kissed like this. Never felt such an intensity of desire that brought her body to urgent life. Her nipples, jutting beneath her clingy top, were so hard they hurt. Between her legs she ached with a need she barely understood.

Her ex-husband had crushed her confidence with his mental cruelty, but now the startling idea occurred to her that perhaps she wasn't frigid, and maybe Calum's inability to make love to her had not been entirely her fault, as he'd claimed.

Paloma was totally absorbed in the sensations that Daniele was creating with his mouth and hands. He feathered his fingertips down her spine and spread his fingers over her bottom. When he hauled her even closer to him, so that her pelvis was flush with his, she caught her breath as she felt the unmistakable ridge of his arousal beneath his shorts.

He lifted his head and his amber eyes burned into her. 'If we act this convincingly in public, we will be in danger of being arrested for indecency,' he drawled.

Of course he was acting, and so was she. The salutary reminder of their marriage bargain doused the fire inside Paloma. She managed a nonchalant shrug when he stepped away from her. 'I guess we will have to suffer a few kisses if it means that we both get what we want.'

His gaze narrowed. 'I apologise if you found kissing me an ordeal.' He walked over to the punchbag suspended from the ceiling and pulled on a pair of boxing gloves. 'I'm going to continue working out.' It was a dismissal. Paloma felt his gaze follow her when she walked towards the door. 'You were an excellent student, by the way.'

She glanced back at him. 'At martial arts or kissing?'

A grin broke across Daniele's stern features and for a moment he looked almost boyish. 'Both, *cara.*'

CHAPTER SIX

THAT KISS WAS branded onto Daniele's psyche and he had thought of little else for the past four days. He'd had a good reason to kiss Paloma, he brooded. Tonight the Morante Foundation's charity ball was to take place at the palazzo, and they would be seen in public for the first time since the news of their engagement had broken in the media, the day after Marcello's funeral.

The funeral had been a small affair. Paloma and Franco were Marcello's only family, and he'd left instructions in his will for a few of his closest friends to attend the ceremony in the private chapel in the grounds of the palazzo. Paloma had been pale but composed, but when Daniele had seen tears slip silently down her cheeks, he'd taken hold of her hand, and she had curled her fingers tightly around his.

The practice kiss at the farmhouse had been necessary. It would be no good if Paloma shrank away from him when they were in front of the curious eyes of the shareholders and the long lenses of the paparazzi photographers, Daniele assured himself. His jaw clenched as his body responded predictably to the memory of Paloma's lithe body pressed up against him. He had felt her nipples as hard as pebbles and heard the soft gasp she'd made when she'd become aware of the burgeoning proof of his arousal. It had taken all his willpower not to tumble her down onto the floor and strip off her sexy gym pants. He had longed to drive his swollen shaft between her thighs and claim his soon-to-be wife. And he'd sensed from Paloma's ardent response to his kiss that she was not as immune to him as she would like him to think.

But if they embarked on a sexual relationship, it would only complicate the situation, Daniele decided. It was crazy how, when he'd made a teasing remark about grandchildren and she had responded that they would not have children, he had pictured a baby with chestnut-brown hair and the bluest eyes—his and Paloma's daughter. He had assumed he would never have a family. At least he had never met a woman who he would want to be the mother of his children and he'd believed he was not cut out for the commitments of marriage and parenthood. He functioned better alone, and there were plenty of attractive women willing to share his bed if he desired company.

Daniele pushed away the idea that a man

could achieve his ambitions, make his fortune and have the world at his feet, but still feel lonely. He walked through the grand rooms of the palazzo where the portraits of generations of the noble Morante family adorned the walls and tried to shrug off the feeling he'd had when he was a boy, that he was not good enough for his mother, and now he was not good enough to marry Paloma.

He halted at the bottom of the magnificent, sweeping staircase and every thought was driven from his mind except for one incontrovertible truth. Paloma was beautiful beyond compare. As Daniele watched her walk gracefully down the stairs, his heart missed a beat and his blood rushed south, making him instantly and embarrassingly hard. If their engagement had been real, there was no way he'd be able to keep his hands off her. He clenched his fists by his sides to avoid temptation as he roamed his gaze over Paloma.

Her white satin ball gown with a black floral design was a dramatic showstopper. The strapless bodice had been designed to push her small breasts high and showed off her slim shoulders and the elegant line of her neck. Her hair was piled on top of her head, with a few loose tendrils framing her delicate jaw. Her hairstyle drew attention to her dazzling diamond drop earrings.

When they had stayed at the farmhouse, she had worn little make-up, and in truth, her exquisite features did not need enhancement. But Paloma must be aware that tonight she would be the focus of attention and her appearance was flawless. A smoky shadow on her eyelids emphasised the deep blue of her eyes, and her lips were coated with a scarlet gloss that gave her the look of a glamorous femme fatale.

Oddly, Daniele preferred the more natural version of Paloma. He suspected that few people got to see the intensely private young woman who had shunned the jet-set lifestyle for which her father, a notorious playboy, had been renowned. But in the wake of her grandfather's death, Paloma was one of the richest women in the world and her life would be spent in a goldfish bowl, the subject of constant public scrutiny.

She halted a few steps above the bottom of the staircase and her face was level with Daniele's. Her glistening red lips curved into a smile that did not quite reach her eyes. 'It's nearly showtime,' she murmured. 'The guests will start arriving in half an hour.'

She held up her left hand so that the light from the chandelier above them caused the diamonds surrounding the sapphire ring to catch fire. 'Thanks to the press statement you gave, the news of our engagement is all over the media.'

'We agreed that it would be better to make

the announcement before tonight's event,' he reminded her.

'I know,' she said heavily. 'But it makes it seem real. Only our engagement isn't real, and neither will our marriage be genuine. I feel guilty that we are playing a huge confidence trick.'

He shrugged. 'It's either that or allow Franco Zambrotta to seize control of Morante Group.'

Colour winged along Paloma's high cheekbones. 'You will also benefit from our marriage bargain.'

'I don't deny that having you as my wife will open doors and give me access to contacts and networking opportunities to further my business interests.' He would no longer be regarded as one of the nouveau riche when he married the granddaughter of a marchese, Daniele thought cynically.

He had been intrigued when he'd skimmed his eyes down the guest list and seen that a new name had been added. The Conte Farnesi had paid a small fortune for the last ticket to the charity ball. Had the news of his engagement to Paloma been the reason his half-brother had decided to attend tonight? Daniele mused.

'I have arranged for us to have a drink before the party starts,' he told Paloma as he opened the door for her to precede him into the drawing room. The butler popped the cork on a bottle of champagne and filled two flutes before with-drawing from the room. Daniele took a velvet box from the mantelpiece and gave it to Paloma. 'Open it,' he instructed when she gave him a puzzled look.

'Oh, it's exquisite,' she murmured. The choker was made of three circles of white gold with dozens of teardrop diamonds attached to each circle.

'I guessed you would wear the earrings your grandfather gave you on your twenty-first birth-day and I had the necklace designed to match them.' Daniele lifted the choker out of the box and stood behind Paloma so that he could fas-ten it around her neck. The diamonds looked breathtaking against her creamy skin, as he'd known they would.

'Thank you,' she murmured. Her eyes met his in the mirror. 'I get the feeling that the necklace is a statement of possession, and perhaps a dem-onstration of your wealth to stop any gossip that you are marrying me for money.'

He looked away from her too perceptive gaze and lifted his glass. 'A toast to the memory of Marcello and to the continued success of Mo-rante Group under your leadership.'

Paloma sipped her champagne before she took a piece of paper out of her handbag. 'I devised a questionnaire for both of us to answer.' At his querying look, she explained, 'We will need to know personal details about each other so that we can make our relationship seem convincing. The first question is, how do you like your coffee? I know the answer. You have yours black with one sugar.'

'And you drink your coffee without milk or sugar.'

'I do in the morning, but in the afternoon I prefer a latte, and before bed I like jasmine tea, decaffeinated. We are supposed to be lovers and you should know these things about me,' she insisted when he frowned.

'If we were lovers, I guarantee you would not want to drink tea when I took you to bed,' he growled. A scarlet stain appeared on Paloma's cheeks. He had never known a woman who blushed so readily, Daniele brooded. Paloma's air of innocence was odd, considering that she had been married.

'What is your favourite food?' she asked quickly.

'Sushi.'

'So is mine. That ties in nicely with our cover story. We need to get the details of our supposed romance straight,' she said when his brows rose. 'It will be easier if we say that we met in London. You were there on business and we met by chance in a bar. For our first date you took me to a sushi restaurant.'

'You have clearly given this a lot of thought.'

'Do you have a better suggestion? We can hardly admit to people that we made a soulless marriage bargain so I can take control of my grandfather's company and you might win your mother's affection.'

Her words hit a nerve. 'What are the other questions?' Daniele asked curtly.

'What about your past relationships?' She grimaced. 'You know that I am divorced. Have you been married?'

'No.'

'Ever come close?'

'Not within a million miles.'

Paloma's long, curling eyelashes swept upwards and her vivid blue eyes searched his face. 'Why do you push people away? Do you shun close relationships because you are afraid of being hurt like you were when your mother abandoned you?'

'Dio! I don't need your amateur psychoanalysis,' he grated. 'It's none of your business that I have never felt an inclination to marry.'

'I am simply trying to find out if you have left a trail of broken hearts behind you and the chances that I will come face to face with an angry ex-girlfriend.'

He shrugged. 'My past relationships tended to finish by mutual agreement, and I remained on good terms with my ex-lovers. It's my turn to ask you a question. Do you have any secrets that—as the man you are going to marry—I should know about?'

She blushed again and became very busy folding up the questionnaire and putting it back into her bag. 'I don't have secrets. Look at the time! We should go to the ballroom to be ready to greet the guests.'

Daniele wondered why Paloma had lied. Her stiletto heels tip-tapped on the marble floor as she hurried out of the room. He went after her and took his phone out of his pocket when he heard it ping. The message was brief and satisfactory.

All arranged for next week. D

So far, the gala ball had been a great success. At the beginning of the evening, champagne cocktails had been served, before the guests filed into the palazzo's formal dining room for a five-course dinner. The fundraising auction had raised a record amount of money for the many charities supported by the Morante Foundation. Now everyone had gathered in the ballroom, where a jazz band was tuning up. Before the dancing got under way, Paloma was preparing to make a speech.

Her nerves jangled as she walked towards the podium. Her grandfather had been a witty and entertaining public speaker, and in so many ways he was a hard act to follow. She felt a pang of grief as memories of Nonno filled her mind. He had entrusted Morante Group to her, and she was determined to run it to the best of her ability when she took control of the company.

The sight of Daniele standing next to the podium made Paloma's pulse leap. He looked devastating in a tuxedo. Even from a distance, she felt the intensity of his glittering amber gaze. He had been at her side all evening and had acted the role of devoted fiancé so convincingly that the other guests were both charmed and fooled by him.

Paloma had found herself responding to his charismatic smile until she'd belatedly remembered that their engagement was fake. She had made an excuse to visit the cloakroom so that she could bring herself under control. Her reflection in the mirror had shown her flushed cheeks and sparkling eyes. She looked like a woman in love, she'd thought disgustedly as she'd run cold water over her wrists. She had spent a few minutes fiddling with her hair, but she could not avoid Daniele for ever. Reapplying scarlet gloss to her lips had given her the illusion of confidence, even though she did not feel it.

'There you are, *carissima*,' he greeted her. He slipped his arm around her waist. 'I was about to send out a search party for you.' To onlookers he was a smiling, relaxed lover, but when he dipped his dark head closer to Paloma, he said tersely, 'Where have you been? I was starting to worry that you had been kidnapped again.'

'No one could break into the palazzo with all the security measures you have put in place. I'm more protected than the Crown Jewels in the Tower of London.'

'It is my duty to keep you safe.'

For some reason, his words rankled. It was silly to wish that Daniele actually cared about her rather than thinking of her as his responsibility. Paloma pinned a smile on her face and stepped onto the podium to address the guests.

'*Signore e signorini…*' she began.

She kept her speech short, first paying a tribute to her grandfather, followed by a résumé of the company's successful year, and a promise that she and her future husband intended to take Morante Group forwards together. 'Do you have anything you would like to add?' she asked Daniele, who was standing on the podium beside her.

She was startled when he caught hold of her hand and lifted it up to his lips. He turned to speak to the captivated audience. 'Most of you know by now that Paloma and I are engaged to be married. I am delighted to announce that our wedding will take place in one week's time in the spectacularly beautiful location of Isola Cappracio.'

Loud applause rang out around the room. 'You can't be serious,' Paloma hissed to Daniele. His smug smile told her that he was. 'How dare you arrange our wedding without consulting me? I can't marry you in a week.'

'You can and you will,' he said implacably. He dipped his head, so his face was centimetres away from hers, and her heart gave a jolt when she realised that he was going to kiss her. 'Remember what we practised,' he murmured.

'You want me to use a Krav Maga technique and punch you?' she asked in a mock-sweet tone.

His sexy smile stole her breath, and she was as helpless as a rag doll when he pulled her closer and angled his mouth over hers. He kissed her with a mastery that made her tremble. In an instant, she forgot where they were, and that his kiss was as fake as his marriage proposal.

Daniele tilted her backwards over his arm, and Paloma slid her hands around his neck and clung to him while he deepened the kiss. Her senses responded to the spicy scent of his aftershave, the scrape of his rough jaw against her delicate skin and the heat of his hands burning through her dress. Time and place ceased to exist. There was only Daniele and the fire inside her that became an inferno as desire swept through her and centred hot and needy between her thighs.

When he finally broke the kiss, Paloma

blinked and was shocked to find that they were standing on the podium in front of hundreds of people. She felt mortified by their very public display. Worse still, she was conscious of the betraying signs of their passion. The hard points of her nipples were visible beneath her satin dress, and there was a smear of scarlet lipstick on Daniele's cheek.

'I've marked you,' she muttered, taking a tissue from her bag and giving it to him. His eyes narrowed so that his expression was hidden behind his thick lashes. He rubbed his face ineffectively. Paloma shook her head. 'Let me do it.' She took the tissue from his fingers and wiped his cheek clean. 'There.' It was strange how the small act seemed as intimate as the kiss itself.

She was thankful when the band started playing and she and Daniele were no longer the focus of attention as the guests moved away from the podium onto the dance floor. 'There must be legal reasons why we can't marry next week.' There was an edge of desperation in her voice. 'I'm sure there must be procedures and paperwork to be sorted out first.' Italian bureaucracy was notoriously long-winded.

'Doubtless you are aware that Isola Cappracio is an independent principality, and different rules regarding marriage apply on the island. I have been a friend of Prince Dragan for many years, since I was his bodyguard when he went on a diplomatic tour to the Middle East. The wedding will take place in the royal castle. The Prince has a highly trained security team, and you will be safe there.'

'You should have asked me first, instead of riding roughshod over what I might want,' she said mutinously. 'It's all happening too fast.' A fake engagement was one thing, but the realisation that in a week from now she would be Daniele's wife sent a surge of panic through Paloma. 'We will divorce when I am twenty-five and I can take control of the company,' she reminded him.

'I have no wish to be married for longer than necessary,' he drawled. 'But be careful what you say in public. You never know who might overhear our conversation.' Daniele indicated with a slight nod of his head to where Franco Zambrotta was standing nearby. 'Our relationship must appear to be real.'

'I suppose that was the reason you kissed me just now,' she muttered, feeling embarrassed when she remembered how eagerly she had responded to him. She tensed as Daniele slipped his hand beneath her chin and tilted her face up to his.

'If I ever meet your ex-husband, take it from me, he will not enjoy the experience,' he said in a dangerously soft voice. 'I kissed you because you are incredibly beautiful, and the truth is that I find you irresistible.'

He strode away while Paloma was too stunned to think of anything to say. Suddenly she was sickened by the charade they were playing, and she was tempted to follow Daniele and tell him that she could not go through with it. But before she could move, one of the trustees and an old friend of her grandfather, Gianluca Orsi, stopped in front of her.

'Marcello would approve that you are to marry Daniele, and Morante Group's board are relieved by your sensible choice of husband.' Gianluca smiled. 'Daniele will keep you safe and prevent another kidnap attempt.'

Paloma chatted to the elderly man for a few minutes, but after he had walked off, she felt puzzled that he'd known about her kidnap ordeal. She had not told anyone what had happened in Mali, and she supposed that Daniele must have told Gianluca. One thing was certain: she would lose the support of the board of trustees if she did not marry Daniele. They believed that Morante Group would be safe with him to guide her, and over the next few months it would be up to her to prove she was a worthy successor to her grandfather.

As for the wedding happening next week, Paloma's heart lurched. She had forgotten that Isola Cappracio was a popular wedding desti-

nation and the process for marrying there was
simpler than in other European countries. The
island was a sovereign state in the Adriatic Sea,
located towards the coast of Croatia. Histori-
cally, Isola Cappracio had been fought over by
Italy and Croatia, until the fourteenth century,
when it became an independent state controlled
by the Da Verano family. However, the principality had continued to have strong links with
Croatia, and the mother of the current ruler,
Prince Dragan, was Croatian.

'My brother is a lucky man.'

The voice came from close by Paloma and
pulled her from her thoughts. She looked uncertainly at the man who she'd noticed had
been watching her and Daniele during dinner.
'Brother?'

'Daniele Berardo is my half-brother,' the man
amended with a faint smile. He was not as tall
or as physically imposing as Daniele, and nothing like as good-looking, but Paloma noticed a
slight similarity between the two men's facial
features. 'I am the Conte Farnesi, but please call
me Stefano,' he said. 'And you of course are
Paloma Morante.' He looked across to the far
side of the ballroom, where Daniele was chatting to some guests. 'I came to the ball hoping
to have a chance to congratulate you and Daniele on your forthcoming marriage.'

Paloma frowned. 'Does he know you are

here? He didn't mention you or suggest that he could introduce you to me.'

Stefano sighed. 'The truth is that I have only met my half-brother a handful of times at social events. I am eight years younger than Daniele, and I guess we have little in common. He made it plain that he has no time for me. I can't really blame him, seeing as I inherited the title that should by rights be his.'

'It's not your fault that your grandfather made you his heir and overlooked his eldest grandson,' Paloma murmured.

'Obviously, Daniele has told you about our family situation. He blames our mother for leaving him behind when he was a child, but the story is more complicated than he knows.' Stefano offered Paloma another tentative smile. 'It is clear to see that you and Daniele are in love. Perhaps marriage will help to soften his attitude towards his family.'

Paloma wondered what Stefano would say if she revealed that Daniele was marrying her in the hope of impressing his mother, who had ignored him for most of his life.

'Can I get you some more champagne?' Stefano offered.

She gave him a rueful smile. 'I have learned from experience that I'm less likely to embarrass myself if I stick to one alcoholic drink in an evening. I was about to go outside for some fresh air.' She glanced around the ballroom. 'Are you here with a wife or partner?'

'To be honest, I am trying to avoid the twin daughters of Visconte Prizzi. My mother has decided that, now I am twenty-eight, I should think of marrying, and she is of the opinion that either of the twins will be a perfect wife for me.' Stefano grimaced. 'If you don't mind, I will accompany you.'

Daniele resisted the urge to look at his watch again. It had only been a couple of minutes since he'd checked the time. He was edgily aware that half an hour had passed since he'd seen Paloma walk through the doors at the far end of the ballroom that led out to the terrace. With her had been the Conte Farnesi.

Daniele gritted his teeth and forced himself to smile at the woman standing beside him. Vanda Prizzi, or possibly she was Venetia—the twins were identical in appearance and the tediousness of their conversation—had been prattling on for what felt like hours. A few years ago, the young woman would not have given him the time of day. But the Prizzi family had suffered badly in the recent financial crash and, cynically, Daniele supposed that a self-made multimillionaire was suddenly an attractive proposition.

'People were *so* surprised by the announcement of your engagement to Paloma Morante,'

Vanda or Venetia trilled. 'I heard that her first marriage was a disaster. It was expected that when she married again she would choose someone with...' She hesitated.

'Blue blood?' Daniele suggested sardonically. As far as he was aware, no one knew that he was related by blood to the aristocratic Farnesi family. His mother never mentioned publicly that she had an older son, and he had kept it secret that she had abandoned him because he was ashamed by her rejection.

The young woman flushed. 'Well, yes, a husband with a title. Papà says that the old Italian families are in danger of disappearing.'

The heir to one particular noble family was likely to disappear very soon, if he had anything to do with it, Daniele brooded as he looked across the ballroom and caught sight of his half-brother dancing with his fiancée. Did Paloma think that Stefano Farnesi was better husband material than a gruff ex-soldier? A marriage between two of the most illustrious aristocratic families would be popular with Morante Group's board of trustees.

Possessiveness was not an emotion Daniele was familiar with, but as he watched Paloma smile at Stefano, cold rage dropped into the pit of his stomach. His half-brother was exactly the type of high-born member of the social elite that Marcello Morante would have been delighted for his granddaughter to marry. Stefano had received the best education at an English public school, and his exquisite manners were the result of his privileged upbringing in Italian high society.

Daniele had joined the army when he was eighteen. While his half-brother had learned how to mix the perfect martini cocktail, he'd trained to use an assault rifle in a combat zone. Since the injury to his leg had put an end to his military career, he had created his own wealth and success using his IT skills, but he was in a different league from Paloma and Stefano, who were old money.

'What is your opinion?' Vanda—Daniele was fairly certain this twin was Vanda—asked him. He realised that he had no idea what she had been talking about.

'I agree, absolutely,' he murmured, guessing from the woman's startled expression that he had given the wrong answer. 'Please, excuse me. I promised the last dance to my fiancée.'

He strode across the ballroom, and his expression must have warned of his foul mood, for Stefano looked distinctly nervous when Daniele clamped his arm around Paloma's waist. 'You seem to be obsessed with taking what is mine,' he said curtly to his half-brother.

'On the contrary, I am delighted by your engagement to Paloma, and I wish you both every happiness.' Stefano gave a stiff nod before he swung round and walked away.

Daniele looked down and his eyes clashed with Paloma's flashing blue gaze. 'Why were you so rude? Your brother is a nice guy.'

Jealousy was a poisoned arrow in Daniele's heart. 'Is that why you slunk out of the ballroom with him earlier? I suppose you appreciate the Conte's air of refinement.'

'I went outside for some air and chatted to Stefano for a few minutes. It was perfectly innocent. You certainly seemed to appreciate Venetia Prizzi's voluptuous charms,' she snapped. 'Your eyes were nearly falling into the front of her dress.'

'Careful, *cara*, or I might think you are jealous,' Daniele drawled. The band struck up the final tune of the evening, a slow, romantic number. He pulled Paloma closer, ignoring the way she held herself rigid. 'Smile, or the guests will think we have had a lovers' tiff.'

She pressed her lips together as if to hold back an angry retort, but her simmering silence spoke volumes. While they danced, Daniele tried not to think of her soft breasts pressed against his chest, and the narrowness of her waist that he could almost span with his hands. He did not want to remember how unbelievably good her mouth had felt beneath his, and how her unguarded response to his kiss had evoked a voracious hunger in the pit of his stomach.

His intense awareness of this woman, and his inexplicable need to be near Paloma and provoke a response from her, was unlike anything he had ever experienced. Daniele sensed she was struggling as much as he was to resist the sexual chemistry that was almost tangible between them. The pulse at the base of Paloma's throat was thudding erratically, and her pupils were deep black pools that mirrored her desire.

The moment the music stopped, she pulled out of his arms and hurried out of the ballroom. In the entrance hall, staff were handing out gift bags to the guests and directing them to their cars lined up outside on the driveway. Daniele eased his way through the crowd and ran up the staircase after Paloma. She glanced over her shoulder and walked faster along the corridor.

'I'm done tonight, Daniele. I don't want to talk to you.'

'A few minutes ago, you were happy to sing the praises of my half-brother.'

She halted in front of her bedroom door. 'Why won't you give Stefano a chance? It's not fair to blame him because your mother chose him over you.'

'Why are you so determined to champion him?' Daniele growled, goaded by the images in his head of Paloma dancing with Stefano.

She had looked happy and relaxed. When she'd smiled at his half-brother, Daniele had felt a sinking sensation in his stomach, the same feeling he'd had when he'd watched his mother drive away all those years ago. 'Perhaps you wish you were going to marry Stefano. After all, he would be a better class of husband,' he said sardonically. 'Unfortunately for you, my half-brother has never been required to work a day in his life, and he knows nothing about running a business like Morante Group.'

Since they had left the farmhouse a few days ago and returned to the palazzo, Daniele had occupied a guest suite along the corridor from Paloma's room. When he strode away from her and opened the door to his suite, she was right behind him.

'I don't want to marry anyone,' she flung at him. Her hands were on her hips and her pretty face was flushed with temper. 'It has nothing to do with class. I don't think you are beneath me because I am from an aristocratic family. I can't help it if you have a hang-up about your perceived social status. And it is not Stefano's fault that your mother loves him but not you.'

Daniele lost it then. Paloma's taunt came too close to a painful truth, and his tight control over his emotions cracked. 'Enough,' he bit out savagely. 'You will marry me and honour the bargain we made.'

Paloma was standing just inside the room. Daniele pushed the door shut and backed her up against it, caging her in with his hands on either side of her head. Her eyes were wide with shock and something else. He recognised her excitement, and his blood thundered in his ears and surged down to his sex.

She had driven him to distraction all evening. Every glance they'd shared, the sensual fragrance of her perfume that had teased his senses when he'd sat beside her at dinner, the melodious sound of her voice that made him think of a cool mountain stream.

'The truth is that we both want this,' he told her thickly, lowering his face towards hers.

She did not deny it, and he felt a tremor run through her when he covered her mouth with his and kissed her with a desperation that, if he had been capable of rational thought, would have appalled him.

CHAPTER SEVEN

HEAT AND FIRE. Just like the other times Daniele had kissed her. But this was not a practice kiss, nor was it a kiss designed to convince the guests in the ballroom that their relationship was the greatest romance since *Gone with the Wind*. This kiss was wild and fierce, with an urgency that sent a shudder of need through Paloma. This kiss was real.

She made a low sound in her throat, a hungry plea for Daniele to deepen the kiss. And when he did, when he thrust his tongue between her lips, she opened her mouth to his demands and kissed him back. The groan he gave was raw, almost feral, and brought her skin out in goosebumps. She answered him with a greedy little moan as he plundered her lips and held her jaw with his fingers to angle her mouth so that it fitted perfectly to his.

Daniele lifted her up and supported her with his hands beneath her bottom. Her back was still pressed against the door. 'Hold on,' he told her hoarsely before he lowered his mouth to the base of her neck and sucked the pulse that throbbed there.

Paloma obeyed him mindlessly, sliding her hands up his chest to grip his shoulders while she wrapped her legs around his thighs. His body was as hard as steel, especially *there* where his arousal was a solid ridge straining beneath his trousers. Molten heat pooled between her legs when he shifted position, bringing her pelvis flush with his.

He must have unzipped her dress without her being aware, and when he tugged the bodice down, her breasts spilled over the top of their satin covering. She was braless, and Daniele's amber eyes gleamed when he stared at her small, pale breasts. 'You are driving me out of my mind,' he rasped, before he bent his head and flicked his tongue over one dusky pink nipple.

She gasped as sensation spiralled through her and thrust her fingers into his hair when he moved across to her other breast. When he drew the taut peak into his mouth and sucked, she sobbed something incomprehensible and felt him smile against her breast.

'Your breasts are as perfect as I imagined them,' Daniele muttered, banishing in an instant Paloma's wish that she were more voluptuous. The tantalising press of his hard arousal against her femininity was proof of his desire.

He pushed her long skirt up so that it bunched at her waist and slipped his hand between her thighs, discovering the drenching evidence of her arousal when he stroked his fingers over the narrow panel of her knickers.

She wanted, wanted… Dimly, Paloma recognised that her lack of experience meant she did not know exactly what it was she wanted. But a powerful instinct took over, and her body knew. A tremor ran through her when he eased her panties aside and ran his finger lightly over her opening. 'Please…' She was unaware that she had spoken out loud until Daniele laughed softly.

'I have every intention of pleasing you, *carissima*. You are so responsive,' he said thickly as he parted her silken folds and pushed his finger into her. The effect was instant and shattering. She had no control over the hot rush of pleasure that spasmed deep in her feminine core and rippled in delicious aftershocks through her entire body. At the moment she climaxed, Paloma gave a sharp cry and then buried her face in his neck as the reality of what had just happened made her want to die of embarrassment. She had acted like a naive virgin, which was exactly what she was.

'You *are* hungry, *mia bellezza*,' Daniele growled. The satisfaction in his voice elicited a faint unease in Paloma. 'I'm hungry for you too. *Dio*, I need to be inside you right now.' He fumbled with the zip on his trousers and swore softly. 'Even though I am impatient, I'm not going to have sex with you up against the door. We will be more comfortable in bed.'

He carried her across the room and deposited her on the silk bedspread. His amber eyes scorched her like flames as he pushed her flat on her back and shoved the yards of satin ball gown up to meet the bodice of her dress that had slipped down to her waist.

Paloma suddenly felt exposed with her breasts bared to his glittering gaze. He moved his eyes down to her tiny black panties that were soaked with her arousal. 'These need to come off.' He curled his fingers around the waistband, and with his other hand, he opened his zip and started to free himself.

But the spell had been broken. The fire inside Paloma turned to ash. Unwanted memories forced their way into her mind, of her ex-husband rolling away from her to the other side of the bed. 'I don't know why it isn't working,' Calum had told her sulkily. 'I've never had a problem with other women.'

Calum had not actually said that it was her fault he couldn't make love to her, but the implication had been devastating for Paloma. She had been sure it was because of something she'd done wrong, or something she should have done.

She'd felt ashamed by her inability to give her husband sexual pleasure.

What if the same thing happened now with Daniele? If he started to have sex with her, but stopped because she did not turn him on, it would be unbearably humiliating. But perhaps worse would be if he did make love to her. How on earth could she explain that she was still a virgin, despite having been married? He would demand to know why, and she would have to admit that she was frigid. Calum had said she was a pretty shell, but her lack of sensuality made her passionless.

'I can't!' The words exploded from her like the ricochet of bullets hitting metal. 'I'm sorry,' she choked. 'I just can't with you.'

Daniele stilled, and his gaze narrowed on her flushed face. He said nothing and the tension in the room stretched her nerves. Finally he let out a ragged breath. 'It is of course your prerogative to say no.' He spoke in a clipped voice, and his movements were jerky as he adjusted his clothes. 'Out of interest, why did you change your mind?'

Conscious of her semi-naked state, Paloma scrambled off the bed and dragged the top of her dress up to cover her breasts. 'We are not in public now, and we don't need to convince anyone that our relationship is real. While we might want to scratch an itch, in the long run it will be better if we keep our marriage strictly as a business arrangement.'

'Scratch an itch?' His eyes had a dangerous glint. 'You know it was more than that. We have been fighting our awareness of each other since Tunisia. A more likely truth is that you decided not to sleep with me because my father's bloodline cannot be traced back over centuries of Italian aristocracy.'

'That had nothing to do with why I asked you to stop.' Paloma was struggling to reach behind her back to fasten her dress. 'Will you zip me up, please?' She turned around so that Daniele could close the zip, and her eyes collided with his hard stare in the mirror. Her reflection showed that she was flushed and rumpled, her hair had come half down from its chignon, and her mouth was reddened from his kisses. Daniele, on the other hand, bore no signs of their frantic passion, and the only emotion she could discern on his stern features was boredom.

'You should return to your room,' he told her coolly. 'And in future I suggest that you are clear in your mind what you want before you invite yourself into my bedroom.'

'In future I won't set foot inside your bedroom ever again,' she snapped, infuriated by his arrogance. Lifting her chin, she marched across the room and exited the suite. Slamming the door behind her was childish, Paloma acknowledged, but it allowed her to vent some of her anger. And yet, when she was in her own room, preparing for bed, her body ached for fulfilment, and there was a yearning regret in her heart for what might have been if only she had not been forced into a marriage bargain with the devil.

Daniele stared out of the window of the helicopter as it flew over the azure Adriatic Sea towards Isola Cappracio. The tall white tower of the royal residence, Castello delle Aquile, dominated the skyline. A few minutes later, the chopper hovered above the castle's red roofs before descending to the helipad in the grounds.

Inexplicably, he felt his heart lurch at the prospect of seeing Paloma again after they had spent three days apart. On the morning following the ball, he had chartered a jet to take them to Isola Cappracio. But after introducing Paloma to Prince Dragan, Daniele had flown to Rome. He'd made the excuse that he had neglected his business lately and there were matters that required his personal attention. In fact, his executive team were dynamic and eager to prove themselves. But he'd hoped that distancing himself from Paloma would give him headspace.

Why had he come on to her with a lack of finesse like a clumsy teenager on a first date? *Dio!* Shame and disbelief at the way he had acted after the ball squirmed in Daniele's stomach.

The nagging ache in his groin was a constant reminder of the hunger Paloma had aroused in him. He knew she had been with him at first. Her soft cries when he'd given her an orgasm still rang in his ears.

But then she had rejected him. It was the first time a woman had resisted his lovemaking, Daniele acknowledged wryly. The truth was that ever since he had been a young soldier he'd never had a problem attracting the opposite sex. And when he'd become a successful business tycoon, women had flocked to him. Money was an aphrodisiac, he thought cynically. But Paloma was wealthy in her own right. Had she turned him down because he did not have a title? He recalled that her first husband had been a barman, and she had said that she had been madly in love with him. Daniele sensed that Paloma's ex had destroyed her self-confidence.

Not for the first time, Daniele wondered how his well-ordered life had become so complicated. He showed his identity pass to the guards on duty outside the imposing door of the castle and they stood aside to allow him to enter. Footsteps rang out on the stone floor of the cavernous entrance hall and he saw Prince Dragan walking towards him. The two men halted, and Daniele bowed his head respectfully. *'Vostra Eccellenza...'* he murmured.

The Prince responded with a cheerful lack of

royal protocol and slapped Daniele's shoulder. 'It is good to see you, old friend. Your trip was successful?'

Daniele recalled his restless nights when sexual frustration for his unwilling fiancée had kept him awake. So much for forgetting Paloma. 'It was,' he lied smoothly.

'You must have been impatient to return to Paloma. It is not surprising when she is so charming and beautiful. Your future wife has delighted everyone at court.'

Jealousy felt like a knife blade in Daniele's gut. Was the Prince delighted by Paloma, and she by him?

Dragan looked at him closely. 'I value our friendship, Daniele. Do you think I would try to steal the woman you love?'

Fortunately, Daniele was saved from having to answer when the tip-tap of stiletto heels heralded Paloma's arrival. He turned his head to watch her descend the grand staircase and could not control his body's reaction to the sight of her. She looked jaw-droppingly sexy in a short, flouncy skirt that showed off her endless legs. Her chestnut hair fell in loose waves around her shoulders. As she came closer, the evocative fragrance she wore stole around him like a sensual cloak. But it was her smile that had the oddest effect on his heart rate.

Paloma reached up to brush her lips over his cheek. 'I missed you, *caro*,' she murmured.

He knew she was acting the role of loving fiancée in front of their host, but, inexplicably, Daniele found himself wishing that they were not caught up in a game of smoke and mirrors. With an effort, he resisted the temptation to haul her into his arms and kiss her properly.

'Tell me more about your e-commerce business,' Prince Dragan said as the three of them walked through the castle. 'I understand that you are diversifying into new areas.'

Daniele nodded, glad of the distraction from his intense awareness of Paloma. 'Six years ago, I established Premio as the first cashback company in Italy. I quickly realised the potential to expand and offer other internet services such as insurance and online payments. My latest venture, Premio Worldwide Bank, is focused on SME banking.' He paused when he saw Paloma's puzzled expression. 'Premio Bank provides loans to small and medium-sized enterprises,' he explained. 'I am especially keen to encourage start-up businesses and support entrepreneurs, just as your grandfather helped me when I set up my first business.'

'I had no idea that you own a bank,' she murmured.

Prince Dragan laughed. 'I can guess why Daniele does not spend time talking about his work to you. Lovers have better things to do, *è vero*? Still, you only have to wait two more days until your wedding.'

When the Prince left them, to attend an official engagement, Paloma turned to Daniele. She was clearly on edge. Her tongue darted over her lower lip. 'Don't be annoyed,' she began.

'That is not an encouraging opening to a conversation, *cara*.'

'While you were away, I was in contact with Stefano, and we spoke on the phone a couple of times.'

Something dark and ugly stirred inside Daniele. 'What reason do you have for striking up a friendship with my half-brother?'

'He told me that neither he nor your mother have received an invitation to our wedding. Stefano did not expect to be invited, but he said that your mother is upset by what she sees as a deliberate snub by you.'

'What did she expect?' Daniele said curtly. 'She has ignored me for most of my life. Indeed, it is not widely known that we are related.'

'I thought the wedding would be a chance for you to repair your relationship with your mother.' Paloma's wide blue eyes searched his face, and he had the uncomfortable feeling that she saw more than he wanted her to. 'Our wedding has been labelled by the media as the society event of the year. Shall I tell you what I think?' She did not wait for him to reply. 'I think you withheld an invitation to your mother to punish her because you believe she abandoned you when you were a child.'

'She *did* abandon me,' Daniele gritted. 'She made it plain that she was ashamed of her marriage to my father and ashamed of me.'

'Stefano thinks you should—'

'*Dio*, I don't give a damn what my half-brother thinks. He is bound to take my mother's side because she stayed with him. He did not watch her get into a car and drive out of his life when he was five years old. Stefano never had to wonder why his mother didn't love him, or why he wasn't good enough for her.'

Daniele broke off, as stunned by his outburst as Paloma clearly was by his loss of control. He never, ever revealed his emotions, not even to himself most of the time. Cool and calm—that was what he prided himself on being. But right now he felt like a clamshell that had been prised open to expose his innermost feelings. 'Why do you care if my mother attends our wedding?' he muttered.

'I think you were traumatised when your mother left, and you will continue to be affected by your past unless you can find answers and understand why she went away.' Paloma hesitated. 'You should talk to her. At least give her a chance to explain her side of the story. I'm asking you to invite her to our wedding, Daniele.'

He frowned. 'I'll ask you again. Why are you concerned about my relationship, or lack of one, with my mother?'

'The truth is that I appreciate everything you have done to help me. If it were not for you, I might have disappeared in Mali...' her voice was unsteady '...perhaps for ever. Without your intervention, Franco would have persuaded the board of trustees to appoint him as my grandfather's successor. The wedding will be an opportunity for you to meet your mother on your terms. At the very least, it can't do any harm to invite her and your brother.' Paloma grimaced. 'And before you accuse me of having designs on Stefano, he is madly in love with a chalet maid he met at a ski resort in Switzerland and intends to marry her with or without your mother's approval.'

Daniele exhaled heavily. 'Very well. I will ask my PA to send the invitations by courier. But I won't be surprised if my mother declines to come.'

Paloma did not seem to hear him. She was leaning over the stone balustrade and looking down to the entrance hall at the glamorous woman who had swept through the door, followed by several footmen weighed down with luggage. The woman's voice was audible from the second floor, and probably through-out the castle.

'You there—be careful with that hatbox. I will hold you personally responsible if my hat for my daughter's wedding is crushed.'

'Oh, God! My mother has arrived.' Paloma glanced at Daniele. 'Lady Coulton likes to be addressed by her title unless she gives permission for you to use her name, Veronica. The only person my mother has ever loved is herself. She married my father for his money, and she has done well financially from her four subsequent marriages and divorces. But she cares about me in her way, and, despite her many failings as a mother, I love her.' Paloma's wide blue eyes held Daniele's gaze. 'You are not the only one who had a less-than-perfect childhood.'

'Why do you love her when by your own ad-mission she was an uninterested mother while you were growing up?' he asked curiously.

'Mama is all I have. My only other family member is my great-uncle Franco, who you think might have been responsible for my kid-napping so that he could seize control of Mo-rante Group.' Paloma's wry smile did not reach her eyes. 'I don't doubt that now I have inher-ited a fortune my mother will want to be my best friend.'

Daniele watched her walk down the stairs to meet her mother and felt a tug in his chest when he remembered that Paloma believed everyone wanted something from her. Including him, his conscience pricked. Marrying her would give him entry to the high ranks of Italian society and put him on a level footing with his mother instead of feeling, as he had for most of his life, that he was beneath her. Paloma had been right when she'd guessed that he hadn't invited Claudia Farnesi to the wedding because he'd wanted her to know how it felt to be rejected, Daniele acknowledged uncomfortably.

'Darling!' Lady Coulton's voice soared to the rafters when she spotted her daughter. 'Forget whatever you are planning to wear at your wedding. I've brought you a dress that will complement my mother-of-the-bride outfit perfectly.'

Her second wedding was a very different occasion from her first, Paloma thought ruefully. She had married Calum in Las Vegas in front of a neon sign and two witnesses whom she had never met before.

'I can't wait for you to be my wife,' Calum had told her. 'We don't need a big wedding with hundreds of guests. Let's go abroad, just you and me.'

Paloma had been flattered by his impatience and had convinced herself that she was in love with him, so she'd agreed to an elopement. By then she had told him that she was an heiress and believed his assurance that he loved her for herself, not her money. But only hours after the wedding ceremony, they'd had their first row when Calum had lost hundreds of dollars in the casino, and he'd been furious when she'd refused to give him more money. He had been too drunk to attempt to make love to her on their wedding night, and that had been the beginning of a nightmare few months as Calum's lies had unravelled.

'Apologies for sounding smug, but I knew the dress would look amazing on you,' Laura said in a satisfied voice.

Paloma dragged her mind from the past and smiled at her friend, who had arrived from England early that morning. 'It's one of your best creations yet. I can't believe you made the dress in three days. You must have sat up all night to finish it.'

'That's what friends are for. Luckily, your measurements haven't changed since I made an outfit for you to wear to Ascot last year and the dress only needed a few alterations.' Laura grinned. 'I can't believe you are getting married in a royal palace, and to the sexiest hunk on the planet. You kept your romance with Daniele Berardo a secret.'

Paloma heard a faint note of hurt in Laura's voice. 'I've known Daniele for years,' she explained quickly. 'He was close to my grandfather. After Nonno died we realised that we... um...have feelings for each other.' She hated lying to her best friend, but Daniele had insisted that, while there was still a threat to her safety from an unknown source, no one must know their relationship was fake.

'It's obvious that you are head over heels in love with your fiancé.' Laura turned away to pick up a pearl-and-diamond tiara from the dressing table and did not see Paloma bite her lip.

She must be a better actress than she'd realised if she had convinced her friend that her feelings for Daniele were genuine. Obviously, she would not be idiotic enough to actually fall in love with him, Paloma assured herself.

Laura placed the tiara on Paloma's head and checked that her chignon was secure. 'You look stunning and chic. Very Jackie Kennedy.'

Paloma studied her reflection in the mirror. The dress was an exquisitely simple design, made from pure white silk, with a high neck and cut-away sleeves that left her shoulders bare. The bodice was fitted over her bust and emphasised her narrow waist before the skirt flowed elegantly to the floor. The only adornments on the dress were tiny diamanté and pearls around the neckline that matched the jewels on the tiara.

'I hope your mother won't make a scene when she discovers you are not in the meringue-like dress she is expecting you to wear,' Laura muttered. 'What was she thinking with that peach-coloured sash and enormous bow?'

'The accessories were to match the colour of her outfit. But Mama has set her sights on a Spanish duke who she met yesterday at a dinner hosted by the Prince. I don't suppose she will take much notice of me.'

Laura went to answer a knock on the door and took delivery of a box from the maid. Inside was a bouquet of white roses and lily of the valley, which she handed to Paloma. 'Elegant and beautiful just like you. Your fiancé has good taste.'

The card attached to the flowers simply had 'Daniele' written in bold handwriting. Paloma stared at his name and imagined him moving the pen over the card with a decisive flourish. Sweet heaven, she was mooning over him like the silly teenager who had once been infatuated with him.

'It's time to go,' Laura told her. 'I'll scoot along to the chapel ahead of you.'

All day there had been the sound of helicopters buzzing above the castle, bringing guests to the wedding. But now dusk was falling, and the air was soft and still when Paloma walked through the castle grounds to the private chapel beside the lake. An ethereal mist hung over the water and added to her sense of unreality that increased even more when she stepped into the porch of the chapel. The inner door was ajar, and she could see the guests seated on chairs on either side of the aisle. On the floor were hundreds of candles lining the path to the altar, their golden flames flickering like fireflies.

The romantic scene made Paloma catch her breath. It was exactly how she would have planned her wedding to a man whom she loved. But this wedding was fake. When she was twenty-five and could take control of Morante Group, she would no longer need to be married to Daniele. A bubble of hysteria rose in her throat when she realised that she would have two divorces under her belt while she was still in her twenties. If she carried on at that rate, she might match her mother's number of failed marriages.

Guilt and confusion froze her feet to the ground. She couldn't go through with this charade of a wedding. It felt wrong to trick people like Laura, who had worked for hours to make her a beautiful dress, or her grandfather's close friend Gianluca Orsi, who'd had tears in his eyes when he'd told her that Marcello had been proud of her. But once again, Paloma could not ignore the likelihood that she would lose control of Nonno's company and his charitable foundation if she did not marry Daniele, who had the support of the board of trustees.

Her mind was spinning, and she half turned to walk out of the chapel when the tall figure of

Prince Dragan joined her in the porch. 'I believe it is usual for couples who are about to marry to suffer from last-minute nerves,' he said gently. 'I've never seen Daniele look so tense, not even when he saved me from a terrorist attack in Egypt.' The Prince's hawkish features broke into a smile. 'He asked me to escort you into the chapel because your father and grandfather are sadly not here. I was unaware that Daniele was a romantic at heart, but he gave specific instructions for the wedding ceremony. The candles were his idea.'

Paloma took another peep through the partially open door and spotted Stefano Farnesi near the back of the chapel. Sitting next to him was an elegant woman who must be Daniele's mother. She could not jilt Daniele at the altar, Paloma acknowledged. It was vital to both of them that the wedding went ahead.

Prince Dragan offered her his arm and opened the door so that they could step into the main part of the chapel. Her eyes flew to Daniele standing in front of the altar. He was resplendent in a midnight-blue suit that moulded his broad shoulders. He turned to face her, and even from a distance, Paloma felt the heat of his amber gaze sizzle through her as she walked towards him to seal their marriage bargain.

CHAPTER EIGHT

DANIELE LEANED BACK in his chair and allowed the hum of conversation and the clink of glasses in the castle's magnificent dining room to wash over him. The wedding dinner had been superb, much vintage champagne had been drunk, and toasts had been made to the bride and groom. Now the reception was coming to an end and some of the guests had moved away from the tables and were standing in groups, chatting. The tinkling sound of laughter drew his attention to Paloma, who was sitting beside him and talking animatedly to her friend Laura on the other side of her.

Paloma. *His wife.* It was odd how easily the two words sat on his tongue, and stranger still that the wedding band on his finger felt as though it belonged there. Daniele gave a slight shake of his head, but he could not forget the mixture of awe and lust that had swept through him when Paloma had walked into the chapel looking so beautiful that he'd clenched his jaw to stop himself from gaping at her like a callow youth with a serious crush. He'd managed to get himself under control for the ceremony, but when the officiant had pronounced them married and invited Daniele to kiss his wife, he'd almost succumbed to a primitive urge to throw Paloma over his shoulder and carry her off to bed.

Heaven knew what her reaction would have been, he thought wryly, remembering how she had used Krav Maga martial arts techniques to attack him at the farmhouse. Daniele doubted that his mother would have been impressed if he'd behaved like a caveman. She would have looked down her elegant nose and disassociated herself from her uncultured eldest son.

He had been surprised when he'd seen Claudia with Stefano Farnesi sitting at the back of the chapel. At dinner they had been seated at a table on the far side of the room and there had not been an opportunity or a desire on Daniele's part for a conversation. Paloma had urged him to talk to his mother, but he did not know what to say to the woman who had been absent for most of his life. The truth, he admitted heavily, was that he felt nervous about meeting his mother, and the possibility that she would reject him again. Inside him there was still the little boy who had watched her drive away.

His phone pinged and he read a message before he leaned towards Paloma. 'Will you excuse me while I go and find somewhere private to make an important business call?' She nodded, and he left the dining room and went into a small sitting room across the hall. A fake wedding was not an excuse to interrupt his ruthless work ethic. Ten minutes later, he pocketed his phone, but as he was about to return to the reception, a woman entered the sitting room.

'Hello, Daniele.'

'Madre.' Daniele's gaze narrowed on his mother's face. Make-up did not disguise the signs of age, or the unexpected vulnerability in her eyes. He had recognised her from a newspaper photo taken at her father Conte Farnesi's funeral. But it was twenty-seven years since Daniele had seen his mother in person and he felt a mixture of emotions. There was anger, but also a deep sadness for lost time that could never be regained.

'Thank you for inviting me to your wedding.' She twisted her hands together. 'You have done well.'

He gave her a sardonic look. 'Does my marriage to the granddaughter of a marchese make me acceptable in high society, and therefore to you?'

She flushed. 'I was not referring to your marriage, although your wife is exquisite and very charming. Paloma introduced herself to me a few minutes ago and said that you had asked to speak to me privately.'

Daniele tensed, realising that Paloma had set up the meeting with his mother. He would make it clear to her that being his wife did not give her the right to interfere in his personal life, he thought grimly.

'I am grateful for the chance to talk to you,' his mother said in a tremulous voice. 'I have followed your career as it has gone from strength to strength. Each time I read about another of your successful enterprises, I wished I could tell you how proud I am of you.'

He shrugged, determined not to be affected by his mother's surprising statement. 'But you have not spoken to me for years. You could have contacted me at my company's offices in Rome or Florence.'

'I did not dare try to speak to you while my father was alive.' When Daniele said nothing, his mother continued shakily, 'It is only now the Conte is dead that I am free to do what my heart has longed to do since I had to leave you when you were a young boy.'

'You *had* to leave?' he questioned harshly. 'Is it not the truth that you chose to walk out of your marriage because your husband could not give you the luxurious lifestyle you had been used to, and you were ashamed of me because my father was a common soldier?'

'That's *not* true.' Claudia clasped her hands together so tightly that the knuckles went white. 'I can guess who told you those lies. Your grandmother Elsa never liked me, and she thought your father had made a mistake by marrying me.'

'It would seem that Nonna Elsa had a point,' Daniele said drily.

'Please, Daniele.' Claudia's shoulders slumped. 'I told myself not to hope that you would listen to me.'

Daniele watched his mother turn towards the door. 'Wait.' He exhaled heavily. 'Come and sit down.' He indicated an armchair, and when she was seated, he lowered himself into the chair opposite her. 'I will listen.'

'My father was a terrible man.' Claudia darted a glance around the room and gave a strained laugh. 'Even though I stood at his graveside, I am still afraid.'

'Of what?'

'Of his ghost. He controlled me for so long that it is hard to believe I am finally free.' She saw Daniele's confused expression. 'I grew up in a gilded cage and the Conte was my jailer. I was expected to make a good marriage to forge a link with another noble family, but one summer while my father was away on business, I met a handsome soldier who was home on leave, and I fell in love.' Claudia sighed. 'When I found out that I was pregnant, I was terrified of the Conte's reaction and relieved when Luigi asked me to marry him. You were born a few months later, but my father was furious and banished me from the family home. I did not care if I never saw him again, but he refused to allow me to see my mother, who I adored.'

'It must have been a difficult situation,' Daniele conceded.

'My marriage was unhappy. Your father spent a lot of time away on military postings, and when he came home, it was soon obvious that we were not suited. I had married to escape the Conte, but when my mother was diagnosed with a terminal illness, I desperately wanted to be with her.'

Claudia wiped her eyes. 'My father gave me an ultimatum. I could return home to nurse my mother if I divorced Luigi and married the man my father had chosen for me. I begged to bring you with me, but he refused. It was a choice that no woman should ever have to make,' she said huskily, 'but I had been conditioned since childhood to be an obedient daughter. My mother needed me. I knew that your father and grandmother loved you, and so I... I left you behind. But it broke my heart to drive away. I hoped the Conte would relent and allow me to see you. When he did eventually permit you to visit, it was another stroke of cruelty. He told me to choose between you and Stefano to be the Farnesi heir.'

'You chose my half-brother,' Daniele said flatly.

'The stipulation was that whichever son I chose would live at the Farnesi estate and the other would be sent away. If I had picked you, my husband and baby son would have been banished from the Conte's house. I could have gone with them, but my mother was still alive, and I couldn't leave her. Motor neurone disease was killing her slowly and horribly. My husband is a kindly man, but weak, which is why the Conte chose him.' Claudia looked beseechingly at Daniele. 'Stefano was just a toddler. I chose the son who needed his mother most. But I wrote to you often, and even though you never replied, I hoped you knew that I loved you.'

Daniele stared at his mother. 'I did not receive one letter from you. It is hard to believe that every letter you say you sent was lost in the post.' His cynical tone made Claudia flinch.

'I wrote to you,' she insisted. 'Until you were eighteen and I learned from a neighbour of your father who I had kept in touch with that you had joined the army and moved away. Your grandmother had died, and I lost any means of contacting you. Years passed, and I read about an upcoming entrepreneur and IT wizard. I wanted to call you, but I was afraid of your response.' A tear slid down her cheek. 'I thought you might hate me, and I couldn't blame you.'

Daniele's mind was reeling. His mother's story sounded genuine, and he was surprised by how badly he wanted to believe her. 'Why didn't I receive your letters? It can only be because you did not send them, and you are lying.'

'I swear I sent them.' Claudia stood up. 'Perhaps Luigi or Elsa did not want you to read them.'

'My father would not have kept them from me,' Daniele said with certainty.

'No, I don't think so. Luigi was not a vindictive man. But I imagine your grandmother's dislike of me increased after I left.'

Daniele remembered that Nonna Elsa had discouraged him from talking about his mother, and she'd had nothing good to say about Claudia Farnesi.

'I'm sorry, *mi figlio*,' his mother whispered. 'If you did not receive my letters, you must have believed that I had abandoned you. But I prayed for you every day, and I will continue to do so for as long as I live.'

Claudia walked out of the room and closed the door quietly behind her. Daniele did not go after her. He did not know what to think. Either she was a liar, or his grandmother, whom he had been deeply fond of, had intervened to prevent him from having any contact with his mother.

How long he sat there alone with his thoughts, he could not say. Eventually he stood up and walked back to the dining room. The guests had gone and there was no sign of Paloma. He caught a glimpse of white on the balcony, and when he stepped outside, he found her leaning against the stone balustrade, her elbows resting on the wall and her chin cupped in her hands.

She was so beautiful. Something inside him cracked and he needed to be close to her, to touch her chestnut hair that she'd let down so that it rippled in silky waves around her shoulders. He ignored the voice in his head that said he'd never needed anyone, certainly not a woman. His mother's revelations had left him feeling raw, and everything he thought he knew about himself, he now questioned.

Paloma turned when she heard his footsteps, and those incredible eyes the colour of lapis lazuli searched his face. 'You spoke to your mother?'

'Yes. Your little ruse worked,' he said drily.

She blushed. 'Are you angry with me?'

He sighed. 'No. I appreciate that you were trying to help.'

'Did it help to talk to her?'

Daniele filled Paloma in on what his mother had told him. 'She could be lying about writing to me regularly throughout my childhood.'

'But if she did send the letters, what happened to them?'

'When Nonna Elsa died, she left instructions in her will that some files she kept locked in a bureau should be handed over to her lawyer. I had no reason to wonder what the files contained, but I'll see what I can find out next week.'

Daniele captured one of Paloma's hands in his and placed his other hand on her waist. She did not pull away, he noted, conscious that his heart was beating faster. 'Will you dance with me?'

She looked puzzled. 'Without music?'

Daniele selected a song from his phone's playlist and propped the device on the balustrade. The smooth jazz number soothed his fraught emotions, but when he drew Paloma closer, she tilted her head and stared up at him.

'The reception has finished and there are no guests who we must convince that our marriage is real. You don't have to dance with me.'

'Yes, I do,' he said gruffly. He wanted to hold her. Wanted a good deal more than to simply *hold* her, if he was honest. But having her in his arms while their bodies swayed in time with the music eased some of his tension—and evoked a different kind of physical tension in him, Daniele acknowledged self-derisively.

He did not understand what was happening to him. He had assumed he would think of his marriage to Paloma as simply another business deal and he was unprepared for the possessiveness that swept through him. Just as inexplicably, he found himself imagining Paloma was his wife for real. He was no good for her, he reminded himself. For so long he'd believed that he had not been good enough for his mother and his heart had turned to stone.

One day Paloma would marry a man who could give her the love she clearly craved and deserved, and she and her husband would have beautiful children and she would be a devoted mother. Daniele pictured a happy family. He felt like a child with his nose pressed against a sweet-shop window, staring enviously at something he would never have and, until now, he'd never thought he wanted.

Dancing with Daniele in the moonlight was dangerous. It made Paloma wish that she were in the arms of a man who loved her, a husband who had married her because he wanted to spend the rest of his life with her. She had thought she could distance her emotions from the wedding ceremony. But when she had stood beside Daniele in the chapel to make their vows, her heart had been thumping.

She had reminded herself that his husky voice when he'd promised to love and cherish her and the warmth in his amber eyes as he'd slid a white-gold wedding ring onto her finger, next to her grandmother's sapphire engagement ring, were a demonstration of his impressive acting skills. It had been the same at the reception when Daniele had dipped his head towards her and listened attentively to what she was saying. In a room full of guests, she'd only had eyes for him.

She did not know why he had followed her onto the balcony or why he'd asked her to dance with him, and she gave up trying to fathom the mind of this enigmatic man. The warmth of his body pressed close against hers entered her bloodstream, and the spicy scent of his aftershave was all around her as they moved in total harmony to the seductive beat of the music. Was the erratic thud of his heart that she could feel when she laid her hand on his chest fake?

A discreet cough from the doorway leading to the dining room broke the magic, and she stepped away from Daniele as one of the castle's footmen explained that he would escort them to the white tower.

'Prince Dragan said it is a tradition for the bride and groom to spend their wedding night in the tower,' Daniele told her when the footman had left them at the bottom of a narrow spiral staircase. 'Our belongings were moved by the staff earlier.'

The stairs seemed to climb up for ever, and

Paloma was breathless when she eventually arrived at the top and stepped into a huge, circular room. The domed ceiling was made of glass and the inky sky and countless glittering stars looked close enough to touch. A four-poster bed was hung with velvet drapes, but the top was open so that the view of the heavens was uninterrupted.

Daniele discovered a large en suite bathroom complete with a roll-top bath. He walked off to explore the rest of the tower but returned minutes later, frowning. 'This is the only bedroom. *Dio*, I'm sorry. The Prince believes our marriage is real, and naturally, he assumed we would share a bed. Don't worry,' he said when he saw Paloma's startled expression. 'I'll sleep on the sofa in the dressing room.'

He strode into the adjoining room and closed the door, leaving Paloma alone in the bedroom that had been designed for romance. In the mirror, the reflection of a virgin bride mocked her. Before they had been disturbed on the balcony, she was sure Daniele had been about to kiss her. There had been pain in his voice when he'd told her what his mother had said. Why would his grandmother have hidden the letters from his mother? Had she believed Daniele would be upset to hear from Claudia Farnesi, or had his grandmother acted out of spite because she'd disliked his mother?

Paloma wanted to offer her sympathy to Daniele after the shocking revelations that had torn his family apart and destroyed his relationship with his mother. She saw in the mirror her enlarged pupils and flushed cheeks and knew she was kidding herself. What she wanted was for Daniele to make love to her. Their marriage must continue until her twenty-fifth birthday, months away, but the pretence of being a happy couple was already becoming a strain. Every time they were in public, and he smiled at her with heart-stopping tenderness or gently brushed a strand of hair off her cheek, she fell further under his spell. Each time he kissed her, she wanted more than his kisses.

Without pausing to think her decision through, she tapped on the door of the dressing room and waited for an agonising few seconds before she let herself into the room just as Daniele emerged from what must be an additional bathroom. His hair was damp, and droplets of water clung to his chest hairs that continued down over his flat abdomen before disappearing beneath the edge of the towel he'd knotted around his waist. His gaze collided with hers, and the flare of hunger that turned his amber eyes to liquid gold reassured Paloma that she was not about to make a fool of herself.

He lifted a brow. 'Is there a problem, *cara*?'

'I need help to unzip my dress.'

'Turn around,' he bade her in a clipped voice as he walked towards her.

She took a deep breath. 'It's a side zip.' She indicated the cleverly disguised zip that started under her arm and ran down to her hip.

Daniele's big chest rose and fell swiftly when he realised that she could undo the zip herself. 'What do you want, Paloma?'

'You,' she whispered.

He shook his head, and Paloma felt heat spread over her face as mortification loomed, thinking he did not want her. 'If I touch you, I can't guarantee I'll be able to stop,' he said tautly. 'It was hard enough when you changed your mind last time.' The flames in his eyes scorched her. 'You have to be sure, *cara*.'

'I am.'

Still he made no move towards her. 'I want to have sex with you. *Dio*.'

His rough laugh made her skin prickle.

'Want does not come near to describing how badly I ache for you. But the situation is already complicated.'

'If we are lovers, it might make things less complicated. It will be easier to convince people that our relationship is genuine.' Inwardly, Paloma could hardly believe she was negotiating the terms of making love with Daniele. Having sex, she corrected herself. Love did not feature in any bargain she made with him. 'Our marriage has a time limit,' she reminded him.

'And we are wasting time talking.' His slow smile set Paloma's pulse racing. Daniele closed the gap between them in one stride, and whether by accident or design, his hand brushed the side of her breast as he slid her zip down.

'You will have to lift the dress over my head,' Paloma told him. The silk felt sensuous against her skin when Daniele gathered the long skirt in his hands and eased the material up her body as she raised her arms in the air. She was momentarily swathed in metres of white silk and could not see his face, but she heard him growl when he uncovered her sheer bra with a delicate floral pattern over the nipples.

'You blow my mind,' he said rawly. 'You have no idea how long I have wanted to do this.' He lowered his head and pressed his mouth to the side of her neck, trailing kisses up to her jaw, and finally slanted his lips over hers. He kissed her until she was mindless and aware only of his potent masculinity as she ran her hands over his naked chest and felt the faint abrasion of his body hairs beneath her palms.

He unfastened her bra and let it fall away from her breasts. *'Perfetto.'* His voice was thick, and the fierce glitter in his eyes sent a shiver of excitement through Paloma. Calum's foreplay had been rushed and perfunctory, but she'd believed—because he'd told her—that it was her fault she had not become aroused.

How was it that Daniele simply had to look at her and molten heat pooled between her legs? He cupped her pale breasts in his darkly tanned hands and rubbed his thumbs across her nipples so that they tightened and a sensation like an electrical current arced down to her pelvis. Any worries she'd had that her body would be unresponsive to his caresses disappeared. She was burning up, and impatient for her first sexual experience at long last. But she was reluctant to admit to Daniele that this was new for her. Talking would mean he'd stop kissing her and doing the wicked things with his hands and mouth that turned her legs to jelly.

Paloma trailed her fingertips over Daniele's stomach until she came to the edge of his towel.

'I want to be naked with you,' he growled in her ear.

She hesitated for a heartbeat before she tugged the towel loose and it slipped to the floor. It was not the first time she had been this close to a naked man, she reminded herself. Daniele's muscular, olive-sheened body was a work of art, but his size caused Paloma to doubt that she could carry through what she had started.

'You can touch me as well as look,' he murmured.

A memory flashed into her mind of her attempts to pleasure Calum and her sense of shame when nothing had happened. What if she was no good at this? Her eyes dropped to Daniele's manhood that was already jutting proudly without her doing a thing. Fascination took over from her reserve and she reached out and ran her finger lightly along his hard ridge that swelled even more to her touch. He drew an audible breath, and she snatched her hand away.

'Did I hurt you?'

'Of course not.' He pulled her into his arms and kissed the hollow beneath her ear. 'You are a sensual siren, *mia bellezza*, and you turn me on more than any woman has ever done.'

He pulled her lacy knickers down her legs and slipped his hand between her thighs, smiling against her mouth when he discovered her slick heat. 'Why are we standing here when there is an enormous bed waiting for us?'

Paloma's heart thudded when he scooped her up in his arms and carried her into the bedroom. He laid her on the sumptuous gold velvet bedspread and knelt above her, his knees straddling her hips. He leaned forwards, his mouth claiming hers in a slow, erotic kiss. He pushed his tongue between her lips and coaxed her response, taking his time to seduce her with skilful caresses so that she relaxed, but at the same time she was aware of an urgent throb deep in her pelvis that she knew instinctively only his possession could assuage.

Daniele trailed his mouth down her throat and décolletage and paused to flick his tongue across one dusky pink nipple and then the other, sending starbursts of delicious sensation down to the heart of her femininity. Paloma let her mind go blank to everything but the insistent need that was building inside her.

She watched him reach into the bedside drawer and take out a condom and could not stop herself from tensing a little when she realised that it was actually going to happen. She was going to have sex with Daniele. She'd idolised him when she was a teenager, and she'd never completely got over her infatuation with him. He had not made promises that he didn't intend to keep or pretended that their marriage was anything more than a business arrangement. She knew she could trust him, and it felt right to make love with him.

He lifted himself over her and supported his weight on one elbow while he skimmed his other hand down over her stomach. His thigh nudged her legs apart and his fingers gently parted her. When he eased one finger into her and then a second, she caught her breath, knowing that his manhood would stretch her even more.

'You are ready for me, *cara*,' he whispered against her lips before he kissed her deeply. He filled her senses: the heat of his body, the spicy scent of his cologne mixed with something indefinable and uniquely him. She felt the press of his erection against her opening, and he must have been aware of her slight hesitancy. 'Have you had many lovers since your first marriage ended?'

Startled by the question, she shook her head. 'N…no.'

Daniele smiled. 'So it's been a while since you have done this. We'll take things slowly to start with,' he assured her as he slipped his hands beneath her bottom and lifted her towards him. His eyes blazed into hers, and Paloma shivered with a mixture of anticipation and slight apprehension. She had often imagined the physical side of having sex for the first time, but she hadn't expected to feel so emotionally overwhelmed. Her heart was pounding as Daniele moved and entered her slowly. He paused before sliding his shaft deeper inside her.

It didn't hurt. She experienced a brief discomfort followed by a sense of being filled by him when he pressed forwards. Paloma did not know what she had expected, but a feeling of completeness stole around her heart, and perhaps more worryingly, she felt a sense of belonging to Daniele. He had been on the periphery of her life for ever, it seemed, and she had been intrigued by him and wished that he would notice her.

He withdrew a little way and thrust into her again, oh, so carefully. Once, twice, each leisurely stroke heightening the restless ache in Paloma's pelvis. She wrapped her legs around his back and arched her hips to meet his thrusts that grew more powerful, more intense as he quickened his pace. The rasp of his breaths told her that his magnificent control had been replaced with a primitive urgency for release. She matched his pace and they moved together in perfect synchrony, two bodies as one, hearts pounding, breathing fractured.

'Come for me, *mia bellezza*,' Daniele said hoarsely.

'I can't.' Tears of frustration filled her eyes. She should have known that she would be no good at this.

'Relax and it will happen.' He slipped his hand between their joined bodies and unerringly found her hidden pleasure spot. She gasped as he held her at the brink before he gave a clever twist of his hand and pleasure exploded deep in her pelvis. It was indescribable, wave after wave of exquisite sensation that rolled through her and caused her vaginal muscles to squeeze and relax in the most incredible orgasm that was far beyond anything she had experienced when she'd pleasured herself.

Daniele waited until the spasms that shook her body subsided before he began to move again. He stared into her eyes as he drove into her with hard, fast thrusts. His jaw was clenched, and the skin was drawn tight over his sharp cheekbones. The realisation that this powerful man was nearing the point of losing control evoked a rush of tenderness in Paloma. She clasped his face in her hands and pulled his lips down onto hers. He groaned into her mouth as he shattered spectacularly, and shudders racked his body.

For a long time afterwards, he remained slumped on top of her, and she buried her face against his neck and tried to ignore her certainty that nothing would ever be the same again, that making love with Daniele had changed her fundamentally.

Eventually he rolled off her and propped himself up on an elbow. 'That was incredible, *cara*,' he said softly. 'You blew me away.' He trailed his fingers over her stomach and lower to her thighs and froze. '*Dio*, there is blood. I must have hurt you.' His eyes darkened with remorse. 'I tried to be gentle, but you were tighter than I'd expected.'

Paloma could feel her face burning with embarrassment. 'It's nothing,' she muttered. But as she shifted across the bed, she saw Daniele's gaze focus on the small bloodstain on the sheet.

'Bleeding after sex should be taken seriously.

I will arrange for you to see a doctor first thing tomorrow.'

'There's no need.' She huffed out a breath. Her conscience pricked that it wasn't fair to allow him to think he had not taken enough care when he'd had sex with her. 'It's quite normal for there to be a little blood after...the first time.'

'The first time?' Daniele stared at her, and the confusion in his eyes changed to a shuttered expression that Paloma could not fathom. '*Madre di Dio!* You can't mean that you were a *virgin?*'

CHAPTER NINE

IT WAS IMPOSSIBLE, Daniele told himself. He would have known that it was Paloma's first time. Surely he would have felt some resistance when he'd entered her. But he had never had sex with a virgin before and he wouldn't know what to expect. The scarlet patch on the sheet was proof of her innocence. An innocence he had unwittingly taken. Guilt cramped in his gut, and he felt angry, *furious*, at her deception.

'But you were married,' he growled, unwilling to accept the truth of that bloodstain.

'My husband was unable to make love to me.' She avoided his gaze. 'Do we have to talk about it? Why does it matter that I hadn't had sex before? It was all right for you, wasn't it?' The uncertainty in her voice and the glimmer of tears in her eyes tugged on Daniele's conscience. Paloma scrambled off the bed. 'I need the bathroom,' she mumbled before she ran across the room, closing the bathroom door behind her with a loud slam.

Daniele raked his fingers through his hair. His experiences when he had been a member of the special forces meant that he was rarely shocked by anything, but he could not get his head around the idea that he was the first man Paloma had given herself to. Why had she decided to bestow the honour on him? For it was an honour, and one that Daniele knew he did not deserve.

He slid out of bed and strode into the dressing room to pull on his trousers. His wife might not want to talk, but he needed answers. He could not risk being naked near her in case his body betrayed his hunger that was more ravenous than ever when he remembered her cries of pleasure as she'd climaxed around him.

When he returned to the bedroom, he found Paloma perched on the edge of the bed. She was swathed in a fluffy white bathrobe that was too big for her slender frame. Her eyes looked suspiciously pink, as if she'd been crying. Daniele fought the urge to pull her into his arms and kiss the crumpled expression from her lips. 'You owe me an explanation,' he said tautly. 'I suggest you start at the beginning.'

She bit her lip. 'To do that, I have to go back three years. Further, in fact, to when I was a teenager and developed a crush on my grandfather's new computer expert. You knew, of course, and I'm grateful that you were kind to me, especially after my father was killed.'

He nodded. 'Your father's death was devastating for Marcello, who lost his only son and heir. But you had lost a parent when you were at a vulnerable age and I knew what that felt like. I will never forget being told that my father was dead. Grief is a lonely place. You were still a child, and I was glad to share my experience if it helped you to come to terms with your loss.'

Paloma sighed. 'I had led a sheltered life in England, mostly at an all-girls boarding school. When I went to university, I'd never had a real boyfriend, and I felt out of my depth when I was asked out on dates. Things never went further than a kiss at the end of the evening.' She gave Daniele a wry look. 'It wasn't just my naivety. Many of the students on the campus knew that I was an heiress, and I was never sure if guys were interested in me or my money. When I became an intern at Morante Group, and met you again, I fantasised that you were attracted to me. But at the ball you insisted it had been a mistake to kiss me. I assumed you had kissed me back out of pity because I didn't have a partner at the party,' she said in a low voice.

Daniele frowned, remembering how he had been unable to resist Paloma's shy advances. He'd kissed her because he had been fiercely aware of her for weeks before the night of the ball. 'I don't see how this has any relevance,' he growled.

'I felt a fool and rushed back to London, determined to forget you. Weeks later, I met Calum, and his flattery was a salve to my dented ego. In hindsight, I should have known that he was too good to be true,' she said bleakly. 'I was eager for romance and Calum was very convincing. He said he had fallen in love with me at first sight. When I told him I was inexperienced, he assured me that he wanted to wait until our wedding night before we had sex so it would be more special. But even though I believed I loved Calum, I hoped you would feel jealous when you heard, as you were bound to do from my grandfather, that I was married.'

'Are you suggesting I was responsible for your marriage that you have admitted was a disaster from the start?' Daniele controlled his temper with an effort. 'You still haven't explained how you were a virgin.'

Paloma blushed. The clues to her innocence had been in front of him, Daniele thought grimly. She hadn't been leading him on after the Morante Foundation charity ball; she had been terrified. Now he understood the reason for her faint hesitancy when he'd taken her to bed tonight. But she had responded to him with a passion that had matched his own and he hadn't guessed that she was a novice.

'Calum was drunk for pretty much the whole of our honeymoon and the marriage was not consummated. When we returned to London and moved into our new house, I hoped things would improve, but the man who had treated me like a princess before the wedding had become distant and withdrawn.' Paloma avoided Daniele's gaze. 'The few times Calum attempted to make love to me were humiliating. I tried everything. Sexy underwear, massage oils.' She blushed. 'I even bought a couple of sex toys. But nothing worked. He said he'd never had a problem before. It was me. I didn't turn him on.'

'Your ex-husband must have been made of stone,' Daniele gritted. 'Just the idea of you using a sex toy is incredibly erotic. Why did you think the problem was your fault?'

'He said it was, and I felt guilty that I couldn't be a proper wife. Things went from bad to worse. Calum often stayed out all night and I suspected that he was having an affair. I suggested we sought marriage counselling or saw a sex therapist. He laughed and said there was nothing wrong with *him*. And then he told me that he was seeing his girlfriend who he'd been in a relationship with before I'd met him, and she was pregnant with his child.' She grimaced. 'I wondered if his conscience had stopped him from having sex with me because he was going to be a father to another woman's baby. But

Calum was the only man I'd ever tried to have sex with, and I believed him when he said I was passionless.'

'*Dio*, if you had responded to me any more passionately, we would have gone up in flames.' Daniele needed a drink. He strode across the room and grabbed the bottle of whisky that had been left on a small table. Paloma shook her head when he offered her a drink. He half filled a glass and took a long sip, feeling the fiery hit of alcohol hit his bloodstream. 'Why did you have sex with me? You made the first move,' he reminded her.

She blushed again. 'Are you saying you were reluctant to make love to me?'

He gave a snort of derision. 'I took you to bed because I was out of my mind with desire. You saw for yourself that you only had to look at me to give me an erection. But why did you give yourself to me?'

'I couldn't bear to wake up in the morning after my second wedding night and *still* be a virgin.'

Daniele clenched his jaw to stop himself from swearing. 'So you used me as a *stud*?' Bile tasted bitter in his throat. He was enraged, believing that he had been manipulated by Paloma. It followed the conversation with his mother when he'd discovered that he had been manipulated by his grandmother Elsa, who he suspected had hidden the letters that Claudia Farnesi said she had sent him during his childhood.

'I would not have had sex with you if I'd been aware that you were a virgin,' he told Paloma curtly.

'Were you lying about it being good for you?' she asked in a low voice. 'You said I was incredible, but I know I'm not.'

'I was not referring to your performance,' he bit out, furious with himself for being affected by the vulnerable expression in her eyes. Daniele vowed to himself that if he ever had the chance he would throttle her ex-husband. 'Sex with you was amazing. But that's not the point. You were dishonest and deceived me.'

'I didn't lie.' She looked away from him. 'I admit I was economical with the truth.'

Daniele drained the whisky in his glass. 'Your grandfather gave me the task of taking care of you, but I have broken my code of honour and integrity by taking your innocence. I thought there was trust between us, but clearly, that is not the case.' It hurt, dammit, that Paloma had kept a huge secret from him. 'You should have told me that you were a virgin, *mia bella, disonesta moglie*,' he said savagely, before he strode into the dressing room and slammed the door behind him.

Paloma's jaw ached from smiling. Thankfully, the wedding brunch hosted by Prince Dragan for those guests who had spent the night at the castle was nearly over. But she doubted she would be able to relax when she and Daniele flew back to Italy by private jet. She had not been alone with him since she'd watched him stride out of the bedroom and they had spent the rest of the night apart. When she'd woken in the morning, Daniele had gone from the tower. He had met her at the door to the orangery and escorted her to the brunch party. Both of them had pretended to be happy newly-weds, but Paloma's heart felt like a lead weight in her chest.

When she'd curled up beneath the covers in that huge bed last night, she'd cried herself to sleep. Her omission to mention she was a virgin had been wrong, she acknowledged. As a result, she had lost Daniele's respect. Honesty was important to him, and he was devastated by the possibility that his grandmother had allowed him to believe his mother hadn't cared about him.

She glanced at him, sitting beside her at the table in the light-filled orangery. He looked gorgeous in pale chinos and a black polo shirt. Dark shades hid his expression and he appeared to be utterly relaxed, while she felt confused and miserable and was desperately trying to conceal her emotional turmoil. Paloma guessed he regretted making love to her, although throughout lunch he'd played the role of attentive husband so well that her heart ached for the connection she had felt between them last night when they had danced on the balcony.

She had foolishly allowed herself to imagine that their marriage was more than a cold-blooded bargain, and when Daniele had made love to her with such tender consideration as well as tumultuous passion, the connection had felt even stronger. But she had been mistaken—again, Paloma thought dismally. Daniele had married her to increase his social status, and he was no different from most other people who wanted something from her because she was an heiress with an aristocratic background.

'Has your husband told you where he is taking you on honeymoon?' Prince Dragan asked. He was sitting opposite Paloma at the table and several times she had been aware of his dark-eyed scrutiny. She hoped he did not notice how she tensed with shock before she forced her muscles to relax and gave a strained smile. A honeymoon was news to her.

'Daniele is keeping the location a secret,' she said in a falsely bright voice.

'It is not a good thing to have secrets in a marriage.' The Prince sounded serious.

'I agree.' Daniele joined the conversation. He draped his arm casually around Paloma's shoulders and she wanted so badly to lean into him and kiss his hard jaw. 'I hope I can be forgiven for planning a surprise for my wife that I believe will make her happy,' he murmured.

Paloma longed to rip off his sunglasses and reveal his expression that might give a clue to his thoughts. Was he sending her an underlying message that he was prepared to forgive her for keeping her virginity a secret? He was impossible to read, she thought despairingly.

'You should have discussed a honeymoon with me. I don't see the need for one,' Paloma told Daniele later when they were driven away from the castle in a car that had the Prince's royal flag flying from the bonnet. Following the wedding, she had intended to return to the palazzo and stay out of the public eye. Her grandfather's death that had made her a hugely wealthy heiress and now her marriage to Italy's foremost entrepreneur had caused a media frenzy. When the car drove through the castle gates, there was a flurry of camera flashbulbs from the waiting paparazzi.

'The board of trustees would think it odd if we did not follow convention and go away for a short honeymoon. Our marriage needs to appear to be real,' Daniele reminded her. His coolness shattered Paloma's fragile hope that he had planned a trip because he genuinely wanted to make her happy, as he had told Prince Dragan. Her expression must have revealed that she felt hurt, for Daniele said curtly, 'We both knew the rules of the game before we started playing.'

As soon as they boarded the plane, he opened his laptop and was evidently engrossed in work for the short flight. Paloma pretended to flick through a magazine, but inside she felt like an emotional pressure cooker. After the plane had landed and they walked towards the domestic flights arrivals hall, she saw through a window a crowd of photographers waiting for them. Her steps slowed and she gave Daniele a despairing look.

'I can't do this. I can't pretend in front of a bunch of journalists that we are madly in love when the truth is that our marriage is a sham.'

'It's all right, *cara*. You won't have to face the cameras.' The unexpected gentleness in his voice tore at Paloma's heart. She did not know what was happening when Daniele led her down a corridor and into a small room. 'Fortunately, you are wearing trousers,' he said, running his eyes over her white culottes that she'd teamed with an ecru-coloured silk top. 'You look very beautiful, by the way. But it could have been a flaw in my plan if you had worn a dress.'

She was even more perplexed when he handed her a motorbike helmet and a leather jacket. 'I assumed we would catch a connecting flight to our honeymoon destination.' It had seemed likely that Daniele had arranged

for them to spend their honeymoon at a fashion-
able resort, perhaps in Monaco or further afield
on one of the Caribbean islands where the paparazzi flocked to snap pictures of celebrities.
Such places were Paloma's idea of hell.

Daniele had pulled on his crash helmet and
there was no chance for her to ask more questions. They exited the airport building through
a back door, and the motorbike was parked outside. She guessed that one of Daniele's ex-army
friends had been involved in the plan that allowed them to drive away from the airport without attracting the media's attention.

Once they left the city, the lush scenery of
Tuscany was spread out as far as the eye could
see. Verdant green fields scattered with scarlet poppies, hints of yellow where the sunflow-
ers were beginning to bloom, groves of gnarled
olive trees and tall cypress trees lining the road-
side like sentinels, all beneath a cobalt-blue sky.
Sitting on the back of the bike, Paloma wrapped
her arms around Daniele's waist and clung to
him tightly while a kaleidoscope of colourful
images flashed past. Her heart lifted even more
when they drew up in front of his farmhouse.
Hidden in a valley between two hills, it had to
be one of the most peaceful places on earth.

'I thought you would appreciate disappearing from public view for a while,' he said when
he opened the door and stood back to allow

her to precede him into the cool hallway. 'If we had gone to a hotel or holiday resort, we would have had the media circus follow us.' He frowned when she did not say anything. 'But if it is too quiet here for your liking, we can go somewhere else.'

Paloma stepped into the kitchen filled with late afternoon sunshine that danced across the terracotta floor tiles. The copper pans on hooks above the range gleamed and the scent of beeswax polish hung in the air. 'I love the farmhouse,' she said softly. 'I can't think of anywhere I'd rather be.' Or anyone she would rather be with. The thought hit her like a thunderbolt and filled her with panic at the realisation that she could so easily fall in love with Daniele.

She quickly moved away from him and filled the coffee machine with water simply so that she had something to occupy her mind and hands, but she was conscious that his speculative gaze lingered on her.

'Good,' he murmured. 'I have always found the serenity of this place cathartic. A lot has happened to you in a short space of time and I'm sure you miss your grandfather. Plus, I can keep you safe here.'

'I am not your responsibility.' She bit her lip. 'Nonno should not have put that on you.'

Daniele shrugged. 'You are my wife and that makes you my responsibility.' He glanced at his watch. 'I have a few things to do. The files you asked to see regarding Morante Group's business structure and reports by the chief operating officer and other department managers are in the sitting room. If you want to take a look through them, I'll try to answer any questions you might have later.'

Her grandfather's company and charitable foundation were the reason she was married to a lump of granite, Paloma reminded herself when she saw the daunting pile of reports on the coffee table. But she was soon engrossed in reading the history of the company, some of which she already knew, of how Marcello Morante had saved the leather goods business and restored the family's fortune from near bankruptcy brought about by his father's wild lifestyle of drinking and gambling. Her great-grandfather and her father, Roberto, must have had similar characters, she thought ruefully. But she took after Nonno, and she was inspired by him. She was prepared to work hard to make sure that Morante Group and the Morante Foundation continued to flourish under her leadership.

Some while later, Paloma's stomach rumbled, and she went to the kitchen to prepare dinner. Through the window, she saw Daniele chopping logs to fuel the range cooker. He had stripped off his shirt, and his tanned torso glistened with sweat as he lifted the axe and swung it down again. His actions were controlled, and with every swing of the axe, his biceps bulged.

Paloma's mouth ran dry as she watched him, remembering how indescribably good it had felt when he'd lowered his muscular body onto her and made love to her with powerful thrusts. Desire flooded hot and urgent between her legs. When Daniele put down the axe and stepped into the kitchen, she was conscious that her pebble-hard nipples were visible beneath her silky top.

She dropped her gaze from his, but not before she'd caught the gleam in his amber eyes. Lion's eyes. For an instant, his face tightened in a predatory expression, before he turned away and picked up a towel to wipe his hands.

'I heard a car earlier,' she mumbled as she concentrated on chopping tomatoes to make a sauce.

'A friend who knows to keep our location secret brought our luggage from the airport. I took your bags upstairs.' He leaned his hip against the table and watched her assemble olives, onions and basil for spaghetti marinara.

'I found some fresh prawns in the fridge that I plan to add to the sauce.'

'You don't have to do all the cooking.'

'I do if I don't want steak and eggs for dinner.' Paloma's heart missed a beat when he suddenly grinned.

'You remembered that my culinary skills are limited.'

She remembered every tiny snippet of information she had gleaned about him. It wasn't much. Daniele was as much of a mystery as he had always been, and the reality that he was almost a stranger hurt more than it should.

'I'll go and shower before dinner.' He sauntered out of the door, and minutes later, Paloma heard the sound of the shower from upstairs. She would *not* picture Daniele naked, or imagine that they were on a real honeymoon, and she would join him in the shower to play out one of her erotic fantasies where she smoothed a bar of soap over every inch of his magnificent body.

'Are you okay?' he asked when he returned to the kitchen. 'You look flushed.'

'It's from the steam when I drained the pasta,' she lied.

He found plates and cutlery and lit a couple of candles that were stuck into the tops of wine bottles. Paloma thought of the grand dining room at the palazzo and the valuable antique silver candelabrum and decided she preferred the rustic farmhouse kitchen, and the soft glow of candlelight that reflected the gleam in Daniele's eyes. Her fierce awareness of him decimated her appetite, and she felt as gauche and tongue-tied as she had been at sixteen, when she'd been torn between hoping he would notice her and praying that he wouldn't. She was thankful when he asked her about the Morante Group's reports, and they discussed business while he ate with evident enjoyment, and she chased a prawn around her plate.

After dinner Daniele went to his study, saying he needed to make a phone call. Paloma headed upstairs, and the discovery that he had put her bags in the guest bedroom deflated her like a popped balloon. Clearly, he did not want her to share the master bedroom with him. When would she accept that he wasn't interested in her? She ran a bath and afterwards got into bed and read for a while, but when she switched off the lamp, she realised that she could not remember anything about the book.

She woke suddenly and opened her eyes to find the room was dark with just a sliver of moonlight poking through a gap in the blind. Her luminous watch revealed that it was two a.m. The house was utterly quiet, but she was sure she had been disturbed by a noise from outside. It had probably been a fox, or maybe a wild boar, Paloma told herself. But then she heard a sound, halfway between a groan and a shout, that made her blood run cold. It had come from across the hallway. Another shout, louder and even more agonised than the first, had her leaping out of bed, convinced that an intruder had broken into the house and was attacking Daniele.

Heart thumping, she crept out of her room. Her eyes had grown accustomed to the darkness, and she saw a pottery vase filled with dried pampas grass on the hall table. She picked up the heavy vase and heard Daniele groan again. What was the intruder, or possibly there were more than one, doing to him? Paloma felt sick with fear as she cautiously opened the bedroom door.

The slats on the blind were open and moonlight slanted across the bed, where Daniele was sprawled. A quick glance showed that there was no one else in the room. She released a shaky breath and walked over to the bed. Daniele was thrashing his head from side to side on the pillow and muttering something incomprehensible.

Paloma put the vase down on the bedside table and shook his shoulder. 'Wake up. You're having a nightmare.'

His eyes flew open, but, although he stared at her, she sensed that he did not see her. He must be trapped in some terrible place in his mind. She touched his face and he reacted instantly, capturing her hands in his and flipping her over so that she landed flat on her back on the bed. He loomed over her, his features drawn into a savage expression, but then he blinked and finally recognised her.

'Paloma? What's going on?' His voice was a low growl.

'I heard you shouting, and I thought you were being attacked by…someone,' she faltered. It occurred to her that he might think she'd come to his room to offer herself to him as she had on their wedding night.

His heavy brows snapped together. 'If you thought there was an intruder, why did you come to my room?'

'To help you, of course.' She saw his gaze flick to the vase of pampas grass.

'Were you planning to tickle an assailant to death?' he bit out. 'It's no laughing matter,' Daniele said harshly when she started to smile. 'You should have run away and hidden in the woods, and when you were safely away from the house, called the police.'

'But your life might have been in danger.'

'And so you risked your life for me.' He didn't seem grateful. His eyes blazed with anger. '*Idiota!* These people are dangerous.'

'What people?'

He exhaled deeply. 'I am certain the Mafia were involved in your kidnapping in Mali, and they probably planted the photographer at the hotel in Tunisia who took the picture of us that appeared in the tabloids to discredit you.'

Paloma's eyes widened. 'But why?'

'Because someone wants to prevent you from

claiming your inheritance—one way or another. I know how organised crime gangs operate. They would think nothing of killing both of us.'

'You had a nightmare.' She wondered if she should mention the noise she'd thought she had heard outside. But she couldn't be sure of what had woken her, and there were probably foxes and other wildlife prowling around the farmhouse at night, Paloma reassured herself.

She became aware that there was only her silk chemise and the thin sheet between their bodies, and almost certainly Daniele slept naked. His hard thighs were pressing her into the mattress, and she felt a dull throb begin deep in her pelvis.

'Can you let me up, please?' she muttered. 'You're squashing me.'

He rolled off her and switched on the bedside lamp. 'I'm sorry if I scared you,' he said gruffly as she sat up.

'What was your nightmare about?'

He raked a hand through his hair. 'I lost a close friend in Afghanistan. Our military base was attacked, and a mortar shell landed in the compound. One minute Gino was standing a few feet away from me, and in the next he'd gone. He died instantly. It could have been me who had been standing in that spot, and for a long time I thought it should have been me. Gino had a wife and two children back home in Italy, but I had no one. If I had stepped into the compound first, his kids would not have had to grow up without their papa.'

'Oh, Daniele,' Paloma whispered. 'You are not responsible for everyone.'

'I was his commanding officer. I should have gone ahead of him.' He shook his head. 'Usually we received intelligence that we were going to come under fire, but that day we heard nothing until the shell exploded.'

'What happened was a terrible tragedy. But I don't believe that no one cared about you. Your grandmother would have been devastated if you'd been killed, especially as your father had died while he was in the army.'

Daniele gave a harsh laugh. 'My grandmother allowed me to believe that my mother had abandoned me. My phone call yesterday evening was to Nonna Elsa's lawyer. She had left instructions that if I ever found out about the letters my mother had sent, they were to be given to me. The lawyer scanned the letters and sent me digital copies.'

'So your mother *did* try to keep in contact with you when you were a child.' Paloma instinctively reached out and put her hand on his arm. She sensed the effort it took him to control his emotions, but she'd heard the rawness in his voice and could only guess how hurt he must feel by his grandmother's betrayal.

He nodded. 'I have you to thank for helping me discover the truth. If you hadn't insisted on inviting my mother to the wedding, I might never have spoken to her.'

Daniele slid a hand beneath her chin and tilted her face up. His amber eyes blazed, but no longer with anger. 'It was dangerous for you to come to my room,' he said thickly.

Paloma was trembling, but not from fear. It was the way Daniele was staring at her as if he wanted to devour her. 'There was no intruder and no danger,' she whispered.

He lowered his head, and she felt his warm breath graze her cheek. 'I am the danger, *cara*,' he warned her before he claimed her mouth in a kiss of savage possession.

CHAPTER TEN

PALOMA WAS SO BEAUTIFUL, and he was coming apart at the seams. He had held it together for years, since he was a kid, but now Daniele found himself wanting things he'd told himself he could not have and did not deserve. He had been haunted by the belief that his life should have been taken instead of Gino's. Two children had grown up fatherless, but nobody would have cared if he had died in Afghanistan.

His grandmother had been dead by then, but instead of leaving his mother's letters for him to read, she had arranged for her deception to continue after her death. He did not understand why Nonna Elsa had prevented his mother from contacting him, and his sense of betrayal felt as if he'd been shot through the heart. Thank God that Paloma had tricked him into meeting Claudia Farnesi.

He broke the kiss and studied his wife. His. Indisputably. She had given herself to him and he felt possessive and something else a lot more complicated that he dared not define. Paloma was light in the darkness. The only person he had confided in about how his mother had abandoned him as a child—or so he'd been led to believe. And now because of Paloma the tight bands that had wrapped around his heart twenty-seven years ago were loosening.

Daniele stared into her eyes, the intense blue of lapis lazuli. *Dio*, she had feared he was being attacked by an intruder and had rushed to save him, armed with a flowerpot. What astonished him the most was that Paloma believed he was worth saving. For the first time since he was five years old, he wondered if maybe she could be right.

'I want to make love to you,' he told her softly, aware of an odd sensation in his chest when she blushed.

'You were angry when you discovered it was my first time with you,' she said in a low voice. 'I assumed it was the reason we are sleeping in separate rooms.'

He sighed. 'I was angry with myself. I had no idea you were so innocent, and if I'd known, I would have been gentler. I thought you might need time to recover, and I didn't want you to feel under pressure to sleep with me.'

'You didn't hurt me.' Her tongue darted over her lips. 'I liked having sex with you.'

Dio! Did she have any idea how gorgeous she

was with a pink flush on her lovely face and her mouth slightly parted in an invitation that made Daniele's heart thunder in his chest? 'This time will be even better,' he promised. And set about proving it.

He pushed away the sheet and heard her in-drawn breath when she saw how aroused he was. She'd had that effect on him for years, and suddenly it was important that he was honest with her.

'Three years ago, I kissed you back because I couldn't resist you,' he said gruffly. 'I had been aware of you all that summer when you were an intern, and I found myself making excuses to visit whichever department you were work-ing in at Morante Group's headquarters. At the ball you looked stunning and sophisticated in a sexy dress, and I couldn't take my eyes off you.'

'If that's true, why did you push me away after one kiss?'

'I knew you'd had too much champagne.' He hesitated. 'I also knew that you saw me as Prince Charming, which I certainly am not. You had hopes and expectations that I couldn't fulfil. I still can't.' It was only fair to warn her.

Something flickered on her face, but it was gone in a flash and her eyes met his gaze steadily. 'You haven't a clue what my hopes are. I don't think I even know any more.' She gave a rueful smile. 'My priority is to take my place as head of Morante Group and the charity foundation, as my grandfather wanted me to do. It's why I married you. In my experience, expectations inevitably lead to disappointment,' she said drily.

Daniele should have been relieved by her words, but bizarrely he wished he could be the man who helped her to realise her dreams. But there was one way he could be certain he would not disappoint her. He caught hold of the hem of her nightgown and pulled it up over her head. Her long hair spilled over her breasts. He threaded his fingers through the silken strands and spread her hair across the pillows before he bent his head and drew one dusky pink nipple into his mouth.

She gave a low cry and arched towards him as his fingers played with her other nipple. Paloma had given him a precious gift, and he wanted to show his appreciation and wonder that she had chosen him in the only way he knew how. This was all for her and, even though his body ached for release, his sole focus was on her pleasure. He claimed her mouth in a slow, sensual kiss and then trailed tender kisses over her throat and décolletage, working his way down her body until he reached the vee of tight chestnut curls at the junction of her thighs.

'Daniele?' she whispered uncertainly.

'Trust me, *piccola*.' He spread her legs wider

and settled himself between them, and then he put his mouth on the sweetest part of her and used his tongue to give her the most intimate caress of all.

She trembled and curled her fingers into his hair, but she didn't try to pull him away and her husky cries were music to his ears. *She was his.* The words beat inside his head and his heart, and he did not know what to make of them.

'I'm going to...' She gasped and shook as she climaxed against his mouth. When Daniele lifted his head, he knew he would never see a more beautiful sight than Paloma spread in front of him, her creamy skin and those rosy nipples that fascinated him, her eyes, wide and intensely blue, and her face flushed with sexual heat. His. And he made her so again, quickly donning protection before he positioned himself over her and surged into her.

It felt as if his shaft were encased in a tight velvet glove. It was the only place he wanted to be. He slipped his hands beneath her bottom and angled her hips so that he could drive deeper, and each thrust took them higher. But he made himself wait, although it nearly killed him. Only when Paloma sobbed his name, and he felt the ripples of her orgasm clench around him, did his control shatter and he followed her over the edge.

When he surfaced a lifetime later, she was

still there, his wife, her gorgeous body wrapped around him and her head resting on his chest. Paloma was there beside him, and for the first time in his life, Daniele felt at peace.

Paloma opened her eyes to find sunshine streaming through the open blind. For a while she lay still and watched dust motes floating in the golden light. She had spent the night in Daniele's bed, and they had made love twice more before falling asleep. Now she was alone, and the doubts that she'd ignored last night crowded her mind.

Sleeping with him had been a bad idea, but it had been inevitable after he'd admitted that he had desired her when she had been a twenty-one-year-old intern. Three years ago, he'd correctly assessed that she could not have handled an affair and he couldn't live up to the romantic ideal she'd had of him. Now they were married, but romance played no part in their marriage bargain.

Daniele had left her to wake up alone. Maybe he was worried that she was still the girl who had worn her heart on her sleeve, even though he had made it clear that all he could offer was great sex. She was determined not to appear needy.

She would always need him. The thought slid into her mind and refused to budge. Daniele had been a reassuring presence in the background of her life since she was a teenager. He was the only person she had cried in front of after her father had been killed because she hadn't wanted to upset her grandfather even more with her grief. Daniele had comforted her, and he had been her ally and protector when she'd needed him.

It was not surprising that she had been in love with him for years. Paloma froze, fighting a dawning truth. Her youthful feelings had not been an infatuation. Age was not a barrier to love. She was in love with Daniele, but he must never guess how she felt when there was no chance he would return her feelings.

It was suddenly important that he did not find her lying in his bed, as if she had nothing better to do than wait for him. She would show him that she was an independent woman, and he did not have to feel responsible for her just because she had lost her virginity to him. And if deep in her heart she was glad it had been Daniele, she wasn't going to admit it to him or herself.

She hurried back to her bedroom, and as she crossed the landing, she smelled the heavenly aroma of coffee wafting up from the kitchen. A sound made her stop in her tracks. Daniele was whistling cheerfully and, it must be said, rather tunelessly. It was such a normal thing, but from

Daniele, the master of self-containment, it was perhaps an indication that he had lowered his guard a fraction.

Heading into her en suite bathroom, she turned on the shower and closed her mind to everything but the feel of the hot spray on her skin. She ran her fingers through her hair to rinse out the shampoo and gave a startled yelp when a pair of big, tanned hands settled on her hips. Daniele nuzzled the base of her throat and moved his lips up to nip her earlobe with his teeth. A quiver ran through her when he cupped her breasts in his palms and pulled her against him so that her back rested on his chest and his arousal nudged the cleft of her bottom. Erotic memories of the previous night filled her mind, and she was shocked by how desperately she wanted him again.

'I prepared breakfast for you,' he murmured. 'But when I carried the tray up to the bedroom, you had gone.'

'Oh, I'd better come now before it gets cold.'

'It's yoghurt and fruit,' he said wryly. 'My capabilities as a cook don't stretch to a—what is it called?—a full English.' He turned her around to face him, and her heart missed a beat when he gave her a sexy grin. His wet hair was slicked back from his face and the dark stubble on his jaw made him look like a pirate.

Paloma caught her breath when he slipped his

hand between her thighs and his fingers found her molten heat. His powerful erection jabbed her belly as he lifted her up and held her against the shower wall. Pushing her legs apart, he entered her with a smooth thrust. 'And now you are full of an Italian,' he murmured, his eyes gleaming wickedly.

She giggled, but soon she was gasping as he took her hard and fast. His urgency matched her own and she dug her fingers into his shoulders as the storm inside her built to a crescendo. His ragged breaths told her he was close, and moments later they climaxed simultaneously. The perfection of the moment and the man brought tears to Paloma's eyes, and she prayed that Daniele would think it was the shower spray running down her face.

'I want to make it clear that we will divorce in the future,' she told him much later, after he had taken her back to bed and they had been too occupied to think of breakfast. Finally they had made it down to the kitchen for lunch, and they were famished and feasting on bread and cheese and tangy olives.

'Have you had enough of me already?' Daniele lifted a brow. 'I did not get that impression when you were being very inventive with a bar of soap in the shower, *cara*.'

Paloma felt herself blush, but kept her gaze locked with his. 'Sleeping together wasn't part of the plan. This—' she waved her hand in the air '—attraction between us won't last.' She needed to remind herself that their marriage was temporary.

Something flickered in his eyes before his thick lashes swept down. 'How can you be so sure?'

'I know your track record with women.' Paloma felt a sharp stab of jealousy as she thought of all the women who had come before her and those who would share his bed after her. She wondered if he would bring them to the farmhouse and spoil them with breakfast in bed, even if it was only yoghurt.

Daniele leaned back in his chair. 'Your birthday is more than six months away and we have to remain married until you are twenty-five. I have learned that life is unpredictable,' he said with emphasis. 'I suggest we enjoy whatever "this" is.'

For as long as it lasts. His unspoken words hovered in the air. Paloma sternly quashed her disappointment that he had not suggested their marriage might continue after she was twenty-five. She did not want to be trapped in a loveless marriage for a second time, she reminded herself. But he was right. No one knew what was around the corner. A few weeks ago, she had been teaching in one of the most deprived parts of Africa. The shocking news of her grandfather's death had turned her life upside down.

'I just wanted you to know that I don't have any expectations,' she told him seriously.

Daniele's eyes narrowed on her face, and he seemed to be about to say something but then changed his mind. 'So we agree to take each day as it comes. I have a plan for the rest of today.'

'Are you going to tell me where we are going?' Paloma asked him a little while later as they strolled through some woodland near to the farmhouse.

'You'll see very soon.' He was as good as his word, and when they emerged from the cool shade of the trees into the warm afternoon sunshine, Paloma heard the unmistakable sound of a waterfall. Daniele led the way along a path that opened out to a rocky area where water gushed into a crystal-clear pool. 'I thought we would swim.'

'I'd love to, but I didn't bring a swimsuit.'

'Nor did I.' He pulled his T-shirt over his head and grinned when Paloma's eyes widened as she watched him strip off his jeans and boxers. 'Your turn to get undressed, *cara*.'

She glanced around her. 'But what if someone sees us?'

'The pool is on my land, and no one will come

here. Have you never swum naked in a wild pool before?'

'No. It will be another first that I can thank you for.' She slipped off her skirt and top and hesitated for a heartbeat before removing her bra and knickers. Daniele scooped her into his arms and strode into the pool with her. 'Oh, God, the water's freezing,' she gasped as he lowered her down.

'I'm curious to know how you plan to thank me,' he whispered in her ear.

She moved her hand down his body and discovered that the chilly temperature of the water had not affected a certain area of his anatomy. 'Like this,' she murmured, and he groaned when she curled her fingers around his manhood.

For the rest of the day, they swam in the pool or stood beneath the waterfall and dried off by lying on the flat rocks that had been warmed by the sun. 'Like lizards,' Paloma commented.

'You are a million times more desirable than a lizard,' Daniele assured her, and he proceeded to show her how much he desired her. She had never seen him so carefree, almost boyish, and she fell in love with him even more.

The afternoon by the pool set a pattern for the days that followed. They spent almost every hour in each other's company, much of the time in bed, although they experimented on the sofa and on the gym mats after a martial arts session, and most memorable of all was when Daniele bent her over the kitchen table and made passionate love to her while the dinner burned and stuck to the saucepan.

Afterwards, they fed each other olives and black grapes and drank good red wine. And they talked endlessly. About Morante Group—the chief operating officer sent daily reports that Paloma discussed with Daniele, and she was glad of his opinions and advice. He told her about his e-commerce company and his determination to help young entrepreneurs become successful, and they discovered a shared commitment to promote the charitable foundation that was Marcello Morante's great legacy.

Sometimes in the quiet stillness of the night, Daniele spoke about Afghanistan while Paloma listened without commenting, knowing he needed to let the blackness inside him pour out. And when he stopped talking and pulled her beneath him, she held him tightly and told him with her body the secrets she kept locked in her heart.

One golden day slipped into another and another, and Paloma lost track of time. It felt as though their Tuscan idyll would never end. She should have known that nothing was for ever.

Daniele watched Paloma moving around the kitchen with her innate grace that captivated him. She was wearing one of his shirts that was too big for her and stopped midway down her slender, golden tanned thighs. The knowledge that she was naked beneath the shirt made his body clench. Desire was a fire smouldering inside him that regularly blazed into an inferno. He wondered when he would grow tired of her. For surely he must? In his experience, sexual attraction always burned out.

She stirred something in a bowl and paused to study a recipe in Daniele's only cookbook that Enrique's wife had given him. He'd never opened the front cover.

'What are you making?' He strolled across the kitchen, more because of his need to be close to Paloma than any real interest in the concoction in the bowl.

'Chocolate mousse.' She dipped a spoon into the mixture and held it against his lips. 'What do you think?'

That you are driving me insane. He kept the thought to himself and licked the mousse off the spoon. 'Delicious, but I prefer the taste of you on my tongue, *cara*.' He was fascinated by the rosy blush that winged along her high cheekbones. 'Who taught you to cook? Your mother?'

Paloma laughed. 'Heavens, no. I told you I studied cordon bleu cookery at a Swiss finishing school that Nonno persuaded me to attend before I went to university. I doubt my mother has ever set a dainty foot inside a kitchen. After she divorced my father, she took me to live in London, and we had several staff, including a cook and butler. Mama blew her divorce settlement from Papa very quickly and just as quickly found herself another rich husband. I grew up thinking that money, not love, was the reason why people married.'

She poured the mousse into glass dishes and put them in the fridge. 'Mama always forgot the dates of the school holidays, and invariably she was away on a cruise when my boarding school shut for the summer break. I used to stay with my friend Laura. Her family have a farm in Yorkshire, and her mother, especially, was always so welcoming and kind to me.'

Daniele suspected that Laura's family had given Paloma the love and attention that she hadn't received from her own parents. 'Neither of our mothers were good role models.'

'At least you now know from your mother's letters that she didn't completely abandon you when you were a boy.'

'It doesn't change the fact that she left me behind. I accept that the situation was complex, and my grandfather was a cruel man.' His jaw hardened. 'But what mother would leave their child?'

Paloma stared at him. 'I know I couldn't. When I have children, I will tell them every day that I love them,' she said in a fierce voice. Her words hung in the air, and she jerked her gaze from Daniele as the atmosphere in the kitchen crackled with awkwardness.

It was not a surprise that she hoped to have children, he acknowledged. Of course she wanted a husband who loved her, babies, a family of her own. But they were not things that he could give her. He liked his freedom, at least that was what he told himself. Lately, he'd wondered if their marriage might continue after Paloma was twenty-five. But hearing her state that she hoped to have a family reminded him that he was not the man for her. Deep down, he would always believe that his mother had left him because she had not loved him enough to fight to keep him. If he hadn't been good enough for his own mother, how could he be good enough for high-born Paloma Morante? And then there was his guilt that Gino had died and he'd lived, when it should have been the other way round. The truth was that he did not deserve Paloma, and she deserved a better man than him.

Paloma's colour was high, and she avoided Daniele's gaze. It occurred to him that perhaps she wanted more from their marriage bargain than she'd let him believe. And why shouldn't she want more than a sexual fling? Unbelievably good though the sex was, he suspected she still clung to the romantic ideals that had made him wary of getting involved with her three years ago.

'Let's visit Lucca this afternoon,' he suggested abruptly. The city was not far away. He needed to clear his head, but he could not do that at the farmhouse with the constant temptation to make love to Paloma. Up until now, he had avoided taking her to public places because of his concern for her safety. But his enquiries into who had been behind her kidnapping had not revealed a link to an organised gang. Paloma seemed as keen as him to leave the farmhouse and ran upstairs to change into suitable clothes for a trip out on the motorbike.

After the seclusion and quiet of the farmhouse, the crowds of people in Lucca's narrow, cobbled streets took some getting used to, although Paloma knew that the city was less of a tourist attraction than Florence or Pisa. Pretty, historic Lucca was famous for its medieval city walls that were broad enough for pedestrians and cyclists to use. She and Daniele climbed the steps and strolled along the tree-lined promenade to admire the views of the city.

His strange mood at the farmhouse seemed to have lifted, but Paloma sensed that they both made an effort to act as though they were enjoying themselves. The Renaissance architecture of

Lucca's many churches was stunning, and another time she would have loved to climb to the top of the Guinigi Tower to visit the roof garden. But she kept picturing Daniele's face when she'd spoken about having children. His barriers had gone up, and she had an awful feeling that he had read her mind and knew she'd daydreamed of having a baby with him.

They ate at a little trattoria that served amazing wood-fired pizza, but Paloma's appetite had deserted her, and she was relieved when Daniele paid the bill and they returned to the bike. Dusk was falling and a soft mist lay over the fields as the motorbike sped along the winding road that led to the farmhouse. Her crash helmet blocked out sounds, and she was unaware that a car was following them until it drew alongside the bike.

Paloma assumed the car meant to overtake, but it suddenly veered so close that it clipped the motorbike's rear wheel. Daniele accelerated, and she clung on to him tightly when the car came alongside again. There was no doubt it was trying to force the bike off the road. The car's blacked-out windows meant that it was impossible to see the driver. The next few miles being chased by the car were terrifying, and Paloma was certain that Daniele would lose control of the bike and they would crash.

They were travelling incredibly fast, but then

he suddenly braked hard and turned the bike through an opening in the hedge and into a field. Paloma looked over her shoulder and saw the car was following them. Daniele was heading towards the copse at the edge of the field. The bike tore into the woods and Paloma closed her eyes, sure they would slam into a tree trunk. But at least the car had been unable to follow them into the trees. Daniele drove on a little further before he cut the bike's engine and they both dismounted.

Paloma's hands were trembling as she pulled off her helmet and she burst into tears. 'Whoever was driving that car could have killed us.'

'I think that was the idea,' Daniele said grimly. He drew her into his arms. 'It's all right, *piccola*. I won't let anyone harm you.'

She stared at him. 'Do you think the lunatic driver was the same person who arranged for me to be kidnapped in Mali?' Fear churned in her stomach when she remembered that Daniele had said he believed an organised crime gang wanted to stop her from claiming her inheritance. 'What are you doing?' she asked when he took out his phone.

'Arranging security measures for when we return to the palazzo. We can't go back to the farmhouse, as it seems that whoever is behind the threats to you is aware of our location.'

Paloma remembered that she'd thought she had heard a noise in the farmhouse courtyard on the night of Daniele's nightmare. 'I'm scared,' she whispered.

Daniele slid his hand beneath her chin and tilted her face up to his. 'Whoever is trying to harm you must know that we are married and believe that, as your husband, I am the sole beneficiary to your fortune. Only you and I know I signed a prenuptial agreement that precludes me from gaining financially from our marriage. Someone wants both of us out of the way.' He held her closer when she shivered. 'I will protect you with my life, if necessary.'

Because you care about me, or because you promised Marcello that you would protect me? Paloma wanted to ask him. But then his dark head swooped down, and he angled his mouth over hers, kissing her fiercely.

Her senses were heightened from the adrenaline that had surged through her when they had been chased on the bike. All that mattered was that they were alive, and she kissed him back unguardedly, unable to hide her emotional response to him.

When he broke off the kiss at last and stared

into her eyes, she trembled anew, thinking she'd glimpsed something in his amber depths that gave her hope that he felt something for her. But there was no time to talk. He pulled on his crash helmet, and she did the same. The journey to the palazzo was thankfully uneventful. There were security guards at the gates, and more patrolling the grounds, Daniele explained when the butler ushered them into the house.

'A bodyguard will drive you to Morante Group's offices tomorrow morning,' Daniele told her. 'I have to go away for a couple of days. I'll inform the police about the incident, but their investigation will take time.'

'Does your trip have anything to do with what happened tonight?' she asked shakily.

He nodded. 'I have contacts from when I was in the special forces and infiltrated a Mafia gang. A couple of people I knew back then became informers, but I have to be careful that I don't put their lives in danger.'

'What about your life being in danger?' Terror gripped Paloma when Daniele strode across the entrance hall towards the front door. 'Is there any point in telling you to take care of yourself?'

He smiled briefly, but he had become an enigmatic stranger once more. 'I suggest you focus on your job running your company, *cara*, and let me do mine.'

With a heavy heart, Paloma realised that first and foremost Daniele regarded her as his responsibility, and the honeymoon was over.

CHAPTER ELEVEN

IT FELT SURREAL to be in her grandfather's office at Morante Group's headquarters, sitting at his desk, in his chair. Tears pricked Paloma's eyes when she picked up a framed photograph of herself taken at her graduation ceremony that Nonno had kept on the desk. She missed him terribly and wished with all her heart that she had moved to Italy after university and worked with him. His business experience would have been invaluable to her, but it was too late to learn from his wisdom and advice. Her grandfather was with his beloved Isabella at last, and Paloma was in charge of his billion-dollar company that employed thousands of staff worldwide.

But she had only been able to claim her position at the head of the company by entering into a marriage bargain with Daniele. For the past two days, she had met each of the board members privately and sought to win their backing for her plan to promote the chief operating officer to the role of CEO while she would be in charge of the charitable foundation. Although she had a master's degree in business, she acknowledged that she lacked the experience to oversee the operations and logistics of the company that were the responsibilities of a CEO.

When she was twenty-five, she would become the chairwoman of Morante Group, as her grandfather had wished. But until then, she still faced a threat from her great-uncle Franco, who wanted to oust her and have himself instated as head of the company. Paloma knew she had to stay married to Daniele for the next six months, but what kind of marriage would they have? He desired her for now, but who knew how long the attraction he felt for her would last?

Her phone rang, and her heart leapt, hoping that he was calling her. 'Laura.' Her disappointment that it was not Daniele on the line quickly faded when she heard her friend's cheerful voice. They had kept in contact with occasional text messages since the wedding.

'How was the honeymoon? It was so romantic that Daniele whisked you away to a secret location. Did you go somewhere exotic?'

'He took me to his farmhouse in Tuscany and it is very beautiful and romantic.' Paloma bit her lip as she remembered long, lazy days when she and Daniele had laughed and talked, and he'd made slow, sensual love to her beneath the shade of the maple tree in the courtyard garden. 'It's no good,' she told Laura in a choked voice. 'I can't keep up the pretence and let you think that my marriage is wonderful when it's all a lie.'

'How do you mean?' Laura asked gently. 'What is a lie? You love Daniele, don't you?'

'God, *yes*! I love him. I wouldn't have agreed to marry him if I didn't love him with all my heart.' The truth hit Paloma with the force of a meteor. She cared about Morante Group, of course, and she was determined to be her grandfather's successor, but she would have found another way to claim her place in the company that did not involve a loveless marriage.

'Daniele doesn't love me, but I hoped he would grow to care for me,' she told Laura on a sob. 'He suggested that we should marry to stop my great-uncle Franco from trying to seize control of the company. Daniele has the support of the board, who were happy that he and I would run Morante Group together for a transition period until my twenty-fifth birthday.'

'But why did Daniele suggest marriage? Unless it was because he wanted to marry you,' Laura said slowly. 'I don't see how a marriage bargain would benefit him. He's very wealthy. A self-made millionaire, I've heard. So it can't be that he was after your money like the weasel you married first time round,' she reassured Paloma.

'He wanted the increased social status that

marrying the granddaughter of a marchese would give him,' Paloma muttered through her tears.

'Are you sure he doesn't return your feelings?'

'Quite sure. He made it clear that it's just about sex for him.'

'It's only that I saw how he looked at you at the wedding. As if he couldn't believe his luck that you had agreed to be his wife. Why don't you ask him if he has feelings for you?'

Paloma sniffed and wiped her hand over her wet eyes. 'What if he says that he doesn't?'

'Well, at least you'll know where you stand,' Laura said in her matter-of-fact manner that brought a rueful smile to Paloma's lips despite her heartache. Her friend made it sound so simple. But if she pushed Daniele for an answer to where their relationship was going, she might lose everything.

For the rest of the day, she focused on work, as Daniele had suggested, and became so absorbed in a report on the Morante Foundation's various charity projects that it was early evening when she stood up and stretched after sitting for hours. The work of the foundation had been important to her grandfather, and she would fight any opposition from Franco, who wanted to reduce the amount of business profits paid into the charity.

Once again, it came back to Daniele, Paloma

thought despondently. She needed him if she were to have the support of the board and shareholders. But she needed him for much more than that. When they had been on their honeymoon, he had made her happy in a thousand different ways.

He really listened when she talked to him, and he'd given her confidence that she could run Morante Group successfully. He made her feel beautiful and desirable, and she had regained a sense of self-worth that Calum had destroyed. She was becoming the woman she had always wanted to be, and when she remembered how relaxed Daniele had been at the farmhouse, she was convinced that she made him happy too.

She was driven back to the palazzo by her bodyguard, Bruno, a burly ex-boxer who had served in the paratrooper regiment with Daniele. 'The boss said that if I allow a single hair on your head to be harmed, he will take me apart limb by limb,' Bruno told her with a grin that did not disguise his obvious respect for Daniele. 'Tell him that Sofia still hasn't had the baby.' At Paloma's questioning look, he explained, 'My wife is a week overdue to give birth to our second child.'

'Daniele is away at the moment.' She felt a stab of concern that she had not heard from him since he'd left the palazzo.

'Your husband arrived home an hour ago,'

Bruno said as he opened the door for her to climb out of the car.

Paloma tore into the house and ran upstairs to her room, intending to change her skirt and blouse that she'd worn to the office for something sexier. But when she opened her wardrobe, it was empty.

The maid came into the room. '*Scusa, signorina.*'

'Where are my clothes?'

'*Il signore* asked me to move your things into his room.'

The master suite had been refurbished eighteen months ago after Marcello had transferred to a bedroom on the ground floor because he'd found climbing the stairs difficult. Paloma barely noticed the sumptuous black-and-gold decor as she heard the shower in the en suite bathroom running. She slipped into the room and caught her breath when she saw Daniele through the misted glass of the shower screen.

He was a work of art. That body of his: lean and powerfully muscular, the broad chest that tapered down to narrow hips and strong thighs. Through the steam, she could make out the whorls of black hairs that grew thickly on his chest and arrowed over his abdomen to the base of his manhood. So absorbed was she in her appreciation of his masculine form that she yelped in shock when he stretched an arm around the screen and caught hold of her shoulder. He tugged and she found herself pulled beneath the spray.

'I'm wearing my clothes,' she protested. Glancing down, she saw that her silk blouse was plastered against her breasts and her nipples had already hardened in anticipation.

'Not for much longer,' Daniele drawled, stripping her with thrilling efficiency. His mouth was on hers, making hungry demands that she returned with demands of her own as their tongues tangled.

'I missed you,' she gasped as he closed his lips around one taut nipple and sucked hard. 'Did you miss me?'

'Can't you tell?' he said thickly, lifting her up so that her pelvis was flush with his and his erection pressed between her thighs. 'I need to be inside you now, *cara*.'

She wanted to ask if he had only missed her for sex, but his urgency heightened her own, and when he slid an exploratory finger inside her, she was slick and ready for him. He replaced his finger with his rock-hard length, entering her with a powerful thrust that drove the breath from her body. She wrapped her legs around his waist, and he cupped her bottom in his hands as he drove into her faster, faster. The intensity was too much, and she gave a cry as her orgasm surged through her in wave after wave of pleasure. Daniele pressed his mouth against her neck, and his groan was muffled when he came hard, shudders racking his big body.

Afterwards, Paloma blasted her hair with the hairdryer and slipped on Daniele's shirt. The musky scent of his cologne clung to the fabric, and she breathed deep before following him into the bedroom. He was wearing slim-fit trousers and was buttoning a black silk shirt. 'I asked for dinner to be served at eight.'

'I'd better get dressed.' She smiled. 'You had my clothes moved to your room.'

'Of course. The staff would think it odd if we did not sleep together, now we are married. We don't want to risk a careless comment reaching the press and Morante Group's shareholders.'

Disappointment twisted in her stomach. 'Is that the only reason you want me to share a room with you?'

Daniele strolled towards her with that easy grace of his that reminded her of a jungle cat. 'I proved a few minutes ago that I want you in my bed every night.' His lazy smile faded, and his eyes narrowed on her tense face. 'Am I missing something, *cara*?'

She bit her lip. 'It's just that I thought... I hoped that what we have between us is more than sex.'

'What we have?' He sounded genuinely

puzzled, and Paloma's hopes sank like a stone dropped into a pool. She snatched a breath.

'I have feelings for you, Daniele. I care about you. Do you feel *anything* for me?'

His shuttered expression told her nothing. 'You know that I care about your welfare. I will protect you—'

'It's not your protection that my heart longs for,' she burst out. 'I want you to love me...as I love you.'

His silence crushed her daydreams and ground them to dust. *At least you'll know where you stand,* Laura had said. Now Paloma knew that she stood alone, as she always had, she thought painfully. Only her grandfather had truly loved her. To claim the company that had meant so much to Nonno, she had married Daniele. But she had committed the unforgivable folly of falling in love with him.

'I was honest with you from the start when I told you that I am not the man to fulfil your hopes and dreams,' he said grimly.

'Is that because you don't want to?' she whispered.

'I can't be the man you want me to be.'

'I want the man you are. Not a different version of you that suits me. Even as a teenager, I never saw you as a fairy-tale Prince Charming. I fell in love with you because you are strong and gentle, fierce and kind.'

A nerve jumping in Daniele's cheek was the only indication that his features had not been carved from granite. 'I have never wanted to fall in love because it doesn't last. What is the point in setting yourself up for disappointment and failure?' He stepped closer to her, but when he placed his hand on her shoulder, she jerked away from him.

'Love doesn't always fail.' Paloma bit her lip at his cynical look. Her family's track record for commitment wasn't impressive, and nor was Daniele's.

'What we have is good,' he insisted. 'Friendship, respect for one another and—'

'Great sex,' she supplied heavily.

His eyes flashed. 'Don't knock it, *cara*. The desire we feel for each other is off the scale.' He dragged her into his arms, ignoring how she held herself stiffly, and threaded his fingers through her hair. 'You won't find such passion with anyone else.'

'It's not enough for me.' She would give up her entire fortune to be able to kiss Daniele's stubbled jaw and have him claim her lips in a kiss that came from his heart. But his heart would never belong to her, and so she eased away from him, and he slowly dropped his arms down to his sides.

'I thought I could be content with a sexual relationship,' she said huskily. 'But you taught me that I deserve better than second best. I deserve love, and one day I know I will find it. I can't make love with you any more and pretend that it's meaningless, that the pleasure I feel when you are inside me is just a physical response. I have to be true to myself. I'll sleep in my own room from now on, and I don't give a damn what the staff make of it.'

Daniele heard the snick of the bedroom door as Paloma closed it quietly behind her. If she'd slammed the door, it would have been easier to dismiss her shocking outburst as overemotional—and emotions on any level were guaranteed to send a shudder through him. But it hadn't been histrionics. He'd heard the hurt in her voice, and he felt guilty that he was responsible.

Dio! She loved *him*. Why, he couldn't imagine. He was not the man for her, and one day she would realise it when she met someone more charming and gracious, someone more suitable for the granddaughter of a marchese than a gruff soldier who saw love for what it was—an illusion.

He ate dinner alone in the grand dining room and asked the housekeeper to take a tray up to his wife, who had a headache and would not be joining him. Was this how things would be from now on? he wondered. Separate meals, separate bedrooms and separate lives.

When Paloma had asked if he had missed her, he'd allowed her to think it had only been sexual frustration that had kept him awake at night. But the truth was that sex was only part of her allure. He liked her smile and her fierce intelligence, her dry sense of humour that caught him off guard, and her boundless compassion and determination to use her fortune to help others. There was a lot of her grandfather in her. Thinking of Marcello reminded Daniele that his old friend had hoped his granddaughter would marry well.

The next morning, Paloma was already sitting at the breakfast table on the terrace when he stepped outside. It was another glorious summer's day, but Daniele did not notice the cobalt-blue sky or hear the cheerful birdsong in the garden. He had the feeling that it would always be winter now. Paloma's coolness made him long for the warmth of her smile.

'Tio Franco has called an extraordinary meeting of the board of trustees and the shareholders to take place this morning. Do you know what it's about?'

'I have no idea.' He watched her pour coffee from the jug and add a sugar cube to the cup before she handed it to him. The simple intimacy of her action evoked an ache in his chest that he assured himself was indigestion. *'Cara...'* he began.

Paloma pushed away her uneaten roll and stood up. 'We should go. The meeting is due to start at nine o'clock.'

She ignored him in the car on the way to the office. Daniele allowed himself to feel righteous indignation. He had never asked for the complication of emotions in what had started out as a marriage bargain, but their relationship had developed into more than a business arrangement, he acknowledged.

Extra chairs had been set out in the boardroom, and there was a tangible sense of curiosity among the shareholders and board members when they took their seats. Daniele collared Franco Zambrotta when he walked into the room. 'What's all this about? The agenda simply states there is an urgent matter to be discussed.'

Franco looked worryingly pleased with himself. 'You'll find out very soon, Berardo. I never understood why Marcello put so much faith in you. His plan to leave the company in the hands of an inexperienced girl could have been disastrous.'

Daniele looked around for Paloma and saw her sitting in the front row. He strode towards the vacant seat a few places along from her. Franco walked to the head of the room and faced the assembly.

'I called this meeting because an extremely serious matter has come to my attention. Namely the conduct of the two people who hold the highest authority in Morante Group that, in my opinion, constitutes moral turpitude.'

'Are you saying you called the meeting to express a personal opinion?' Daniele asked curtly. He glanced across to Paloma and guessed from her frown that she felt as perplexed as him by Franco's statement.

'I believe it is an opinion that most people in the room will share after hearing the recording I am about to play.' Franco was holding a tablet and Paloma's voice suddenly emerged from the speakers around the room.

'I can't keep up the pretence and let you think that my marriage is wonderful when it's all a lie.'

'Wait a minute.' Paloma jumped to her feet. 'How did you get hold of a conversation that took place on my personal mobile phone? I demand you turn the recording off.'

Franco ignored her plea, and another voice that Daniele recognised belonged to Paloma's friend Laura came through the speakers.

'What is a lie? You love Daniele, don't you?'

'God, yes! I love him. I wouldn't have agreed to marry him if I didn't love him with all my heart.'

'That's enough, Zambrotta. Turn the damn thing off.'

Daniele saw that Paloma had paled, and her stricken expression made him want to sweep her into his arms and carry her out of the meeting. Her voice from the speakers reverberated around the room and inside his head.

'Daniele doesn't love me, but I hoped he would grow to care for me. He suggested that we should marry to stop my great-uncle Franco from trying to seize control of the company.'

Paloma made a muffled sound. 'Please, Tio Franco, turn it off.'

'I think we have all heard enough,' Franco said smoothly. 'It is clear that the marriage between Daniele Berardo and Paloma was a deliberate ploy to mislead the board and shareholders. I believe the trustees have no option but to terminate Berardo's position on the board and replace Paloma with myself at the head of Morante Group with immediate effect.'

'Not so fast.' Daniele leapt to his feet and turned to face the crowded room. 'I will tell you exactly why I married my wife.'

CHAPTER TWELVE

'IT'S QUITE SIMPLE,' Daniele told his captivated audience.

And it struck him like a thunderbolt that it *was* simple. He loved Paloma. But he had fought his feelings and denied them to himself and to her because he *really* did not want to fall in love. He had numerous examples of how love was transient. His parents' doomed marriage, his mother, who had left him when he was a child, his grandmother, who had lied to him. Only a fool would fall in love. Or a man whose heart was pounding so hard in his chest as his gaze sought the intensely blue eyes of the love of his life. Paloma. His wife.

'I married Paloma for one reason only. I fell in love with her.' He wondered why she looked away from him. Addressing the shareholders again, he continued, 'The phone recording has made me realise that I did not make it clear to her how much she means to me. But I hope she understands that I would give my life for her.'

'Don't!'

Paloma stood up, and Daniele's heart cracked open when he saw tears streaming down her face. 'I know what you're trying to do.' Her lips quivered and black tracks of mascara ran down her face. She was a heartbreakingly beautiful mess. He took a step towards her, but she spun around and ran out of the boardroom.

She had lost everything. The realisation made Paloma feel sick. Her grandfather's company, the charitable foundation, the support of the trustees. But worst and most devastating by far was that she had lost Daniele. You couldn't lose what you had never had, her brain reminded her. *Oh, God!*

She dropped her hands away from her face and forced herself to breathe as the car drew up outside the palazzo and the driver, Bruno, came round and opened her door. In the midst of her agony, she noticed that he looked tense.

'My wife is in labour,' he told her. 'Apparently it's happening very quickly. Sofia's mother is driving her to the hospital.'

'What are you doing here? Go to your wife and baby.'

'Are you sure you won't need me to drive you somewhere?'

'Go!'

Bruno needed no persuading. Paloma ran into

the house and up to the master bedroom that she would never share with Daniele. She packed a small suitcase and scrolled through her phone, searching for the next available flight to England. She had sent a frantic text to Laura explaining that her marriage was over.

The car her grandfather had bought her a few years ago was parked in the garage. She was backing it onto the driveway when a taxi swept through the gates. Paloma's heart missed a beat when Daniele got out and strode towards her. She could not face him after her public humiliation at the shareholders' meeting. How Franco had recorded her phone conversation with Laura was a mystery. The memory of hearing her voice through the speakers stating her love for Daniele sent a shudder of embarrassment through Paloma. But even though she had lost everything that mattered to her, there was a sense of relief that she had found the courage to be honest about how she felt. There was no shame in falling in love. Just heartache.

She gripped the steering wheel tightly when Daniele leaned down so that his head was level with the car's open window. 'I'm going to stay with Laura in London,' she said before he asked.

He looked slightly stunned. 'Did you hear what I said in the boardroom?'

'Of course I heard. Everyone there did, but

that was the point, wasn't it? I suppose I should thank you.'

His amber eyes flashed. 'Thank me for what? *Dio*,' he growled, his control clearly under strain. 'Will you get out of the car so that we can talk properly?'

'No. I don't want to talk. There's no point. I know you said all that stuff about being in love with me to try to convince the trustees and shareholders that our marriage is genuine. But I can't live a lie any more. We both know you will never love me.' Tears brimmed in her eyes. She could not bear to break down in front of him. 'I have to go.' She bit her lip when he did not move away from the car. His expression was shuttered as always. 'You have to let me go, Daniele.'

'Is that what you want?' His voice sounded odd, as if he had swallowed broken glass.

Paloma stared through the windscreen. 'Yes.'

Daniele stood up straight and dropped his hand down from the car. 'Then go, *mio piccola*.'

Why had he called her his little one, and sounded so wrecked, as if she had ripped his heart out? It must have been her imagination. Daniele did not have a heart. Paloma wiped her eyes and concentrated on the road. The traffic was busy on the way to the airport. She drove for a few miles on the highway and noticed that a black car was close behind. She kept glancing in her rear-view mirror and became convinced that she was being followed.

Fear cramped in her stomach at the memory of when a car had tried to force the motorbike off the road. She had been so desperate to leave the palazzo that she'd forgotten the threat to her safety, especially as she was without a bodyguard. Making a quick decision, she left the highway at the next junction and sped down a lane leading to a village. The black car was some way behind her. She shot down a side road and pulled over, relieved when she saw her pursuer drive past the turning to the road. Her hands shook as she fumbled in her handbag for her phone. There was only one person she wanted to call.

'*Cara?*'

'Daniele, I'm being followed. It could be the same people who tried to run us off the road near the farmhouse.' Paloma's fragile composure cracked. 'Suppose they try to kidnap me?'

'It's all right. You are safe. The threat to you is over,' Daniele said quickly. 'The kidnappers have been arrested. The leader of the criminal gang is a man called Alberto Facchetti, who is the board member Gianluca Orsi's son-in-law. Gianluca knew the contents of your grandfather's will and he let slip to Facchetti that if you died, the fortune you had inherited from Marcello would be split between the trustees. I guess that after Gianluca had received his share of the money, his son-in-law planned to get rid of him too. I remembered Facchetti's name from when I'd foiled the Mafia plot to kidnap Marcello years ago.' He paused. 'I planned to tell you all of this, but when I got back to the palazzo, I was shocked that you were leaving me.'

'So who has been following me?' Paloma asked shakily.

Daniele hesitated. 'Purely for my peace of mind, I asked one of my security guys to make sure you arrived at the airport safely.'

'Because my grandfather asked you to protect me,' she muttered.

'I would gladly spend the rest of my life taking care of you,' Daniele said roughly. 'There is more to tell you. When your great-uncle Franco learned of the threats against you and the suspicion that he was behind your kidnapping in Mali, he was horrified that you could think he would want to harm you. He is deeply sorry that he had bugged your office and has given an assurance that he will destroy the recording of your phone conversation. Franco withdrew his bid to become the head of Morante Group, and the trustees and shareholders have agreed that you will be your grandfather's successor immediately. I will retain my place as a life-long member of the board and act as your advisor if you want me to. It all means that you do not have to stay married to me. We can divorce and you will be free to fall in love and find the happiness you deserve.'

Paloma gripped her phone tightly. Tears slid silently down her face. Was this goodbye? Would she ever see Daniele again? 'The things you said at the meeting...'

'Every word came from my heart, *cara*.'

After Daniele had cut the call, he'd switched off his phone. Paloma's silence had told him that he'd lost her, and he would not put himself through the additional torture of hoping she would call back. When he had watched her drive away from the palazzo, he'd felt like the five-year-old boy who had wept when his mother had left.

Being at the palazzo had been unbearable without Paloma, and he had jumped onto the motorbike immediately after she had gone. But it was no better at the farmhouse, where memories of her were everywhere. He lost track of time while he was wrapped up in his thoughts of what a fool he had been to realise too late what she meant to him. He stepped out of the kitchen into the courtyard. The sun was fiercely bright. He should have worn sunglasses. His eyes were streaming. He pinched the bridge of his nose and swallowed the lump that had lodged in his throat. He was a grown man, a tough soldier, and he should not be crying, but he could not stop the tears that seeped from beneath his eyelashes.

Dio, he was in hell. He thought he heard a car, but no one ever came here. The farmhouse had been his sanctuary, but he would sell it. Move on. Get over her.

Sure he would.

He roared like a beast in pain. *'Paloma!'*

'Daniele.'

He turned slowly and knew he had lost it completely. Paloma could not be standing in the courtyard, a vision of beauty in a buttercup-yellow dress, with her hair falling in a silky curtain around her shoulders. 'You…you came back.'

'You sounded…' She stared at his wet face. 'Are you hurt?'

'I'm in agony.' He strode towards her, and his heart kicked because she was real, not a vision in his imagination. 'I stood in front of a room full of people and laid my heart on the line. And you left me,' he said rawly.

A tear slipped down her cheek. 'I thought you said…those things…to convince the trustees. It was part of the game we have been playing.'

He shook his head. 'It was never a game, although I tried telling myself I was doing you a favour by marrying you so that you could claim your place at the company.' Daniele lifted his hand and touched her hair to make sure she was real. 'I was in the ambulance with your grandfather when he died. He gave me your grandmother's engagement ring and told me to keep it with me and give it to the woman who captured my heart. You did that a long time ago, *cara*, but I was too afraid to admit that I loved you. I was afraid that love wouldn't last, and you would leave.' He swallowed. 'And you did.'

'I came back.' Paloma stepped closer to Daniele and stared at his face ravaged by pain. He had said he was in agony, and it was there in the bleakness of his eyes, the trails of moisture on his cheeks. 'You really love me,' she whispered in awe. He had said he was afraid, and she understood that fear. Love was scary. It took courage to risk your heart and soul, but she knew she was brave enough and strong enough to love this strong, brave man.

'I love you, and you love me, so why are we both crying, my darling?'

Light flared in his eyes, hope and adoration that made Paloma tremble.

'Tesoro.' Daniele's voice cracked as he wrapped his arms around her and hauled her against his big chest, where his heart was thundering. *'Ti amo, ti adoro, mio cuore.'*

He rested his brow against hers and simply held her, and their two hearts beat as one. And then he kissed her reverently and with so much love that more tears slipped down Paloma's cheeks.

'Tears of joy,' she told him softly. 'My heart belongs to you, and I will never take it away. It is yours for ever, my love.'

'Show me,' Daniele murmured when he carried her into the farmhouse and up to the bedroom. They showed each other with tender kisses that became fiercer and more urgent as passion caught light and became an inferno.

Love that they both knew would last a lifetime.

EPILOGUE

'OUR FIRST WEDDING ANNIVERSARY.' Paloma smiled at her husband, and her heart missed a beat when Daniele's handsome face broke into a broad smile.

He smiled a lot these days. Gone was the enigmatic man who had kept her at a distance. He shared his thoughts and hopes and fears with her as she did with him. But most of all they shared a love that grew stronger every day.

'Next year I'm going to take you away for a private anniversary celebration,' Daniele told her. 'Just the three of us.' He looked down at the baby boy Paloma was cradling in her arms and his smile became so tender that tears pricked her eyes. They both adored little Luigi, who had arrived a month ago with minimal fuss. Paloma was grateful that she had everything she wanted most in the world—love and a family of her own. Luigi's birth had brought their extended family together.

She looked across the airy sitting room to

where the baby's two grandmothers were sitting and chatting. Her mother had descended on the palazzo with enough luggage to stay for a year, although she was only visiting for a week, and a new husband, the Spanish duke she had met at Paloma and Daniele's wedding.

Claudia Farnesi was now a regular visitor at the palazzo, as was Daniele's half-brother, Stefano, who had recently married his pretty chalet maid. Daniele's relationship with his mother was a gradual process, but baby Luigi had helped break the ice. Paloma had decided to work part-time so that she could be with her baby son as much as possible, and she had made Franco joint head of Morante Group. He had been deeply upset that she'd believed he could have been behind her kidnap ordeal, and now he was her firm ally and business advisor, which allowed Daniele to concentrate on his own hugely successful business.

Luigi was asleep, and she laid him in his crib. Daniele caught hold of her hand and led her out onto the balcony, where they were alone.

'Happy anniversary, *tesoro mio*,' he said softly as he opened a small velvet box. Inside was an exquisite sapphire-and-diamond eternity ring that perfectly matched her engagement ring. 'I will love you for eternity.'

* * * * *

If you were captivated by
The Italian's Bargain for His Bride,
why not dive into these other
Chantelle Shaw stories?

Proof of Their Forbidden Night
Her Wedding Night Negotiation
Housekeeper in the Headlines
The Greek Wedding She Never Had
Nine Months to Tame the Tycoon

Available now!